THE BETA'S PRICE

Bakker, Em J. (author)
The Beta's Price ISBN 978-1-7645575-0-4 (paperback)
FICTION | PARANORMAL ROMANCE

Typesetting Garamond Regular 12/15
Cover & Book Design: Em J. Bakker
Cover image: Catherine Highton

THE BETA'S PRICE

PRICE

A Novella in The Queen Series

EM J BAKKER

Northern Realm
Frost Fang Pack
Iron Blow Pack
Atticus Starr Pack
Greyfall
Ravenhill Pack
Dreamshire Pack
Crystal Lake Pack
Sixth Body Pack
Whispering Night Pack
Southern Realm

Chapter One

TOM

ACROSS FROM ME, HELIOS rolls his shoulders, settling into his stance. Too calm. Everything has been too calm.

No challengers.

No retaliation.

No noise from the north.

It feels wrong.

Dawn has barely touched the realm, and yet Greyfall warriors are up and hard at work.

Growls and snarls echo across the courtyard, with fighters trying their hardest to render their opponents incapable of continuing by forcing their submission.

The overthrow of the throne has been a battle hard won, and now we continue to throw every effort of ourselves into training to defeat any enemy to the new king, our king, Helios.

My breath mists in the air, curling visibly like smoke. Rolling my shoulders together once, my joints protest and crack with a satisfying grind, loosening up the muscles and preparing myself once again. Across from me, my opponent, King Helios, continues readying himself, readjusting his stance for our next bout.

It's funny how memories sneak up on a person. One moment I'm standing in the Greyfall courtyard, breath steaming in the cool morning air. The next, I'm there again. Years ago. Cold.

Starving.

Alone.

Back when Greyfall was different. Harder. Harsher.

Everything was grey, frozen over. Greyfall really lived up to its name: a dirty, snow-covered city. Soundless and dreary. I remember it so clearly.

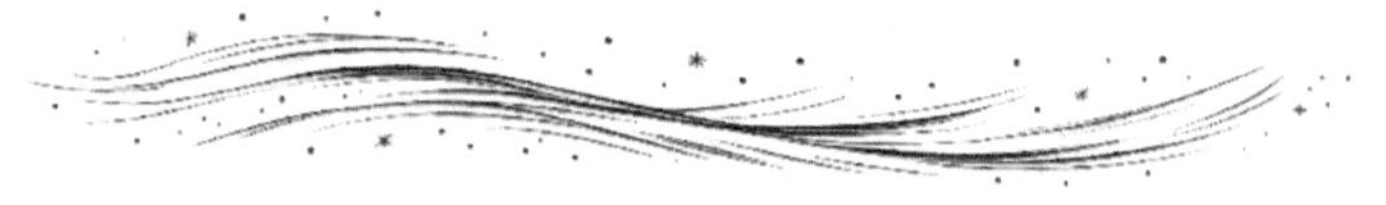

I'm perched on top of the blacksmith's shop, keeping warm crouched behind the chimney. Watching the street below me like the feral little Lycan I was. My stomach was aching constantly with hunger, but my wolf, Lex, was quiet. Abnormally curious and alert.

Then I saw him, a boy not much older than myself, wrapped up firmly in furs to protect him from the cold. Helios, Prince to the death dealer King. Even as a young orphan, I knew his name and his status. He walked older than his years, like someone who never had to look over his shoulder. Like no one could or would ever touch the future king.

He had no guards and no visible weapon, just a cold confidence which I guess comes with the royal arrogance. Be that as it may, he didn't belong out there, not where the cold bites so deep and where the shadows themselves had sharp teeth.

And yet, I couldn't look away from him; an almost magnetic pull seemed to surround us. Lex was incredibly watchful of him.

I received Lex early, after being orphaned, and as I watched the Prince, Lex's attentiveness didn't sway and it didn't go unnoticed by me. Almost like he recognised him, the need for the prince to be safe, I thought.

Then, the scent in the air changed. Rotting, bloody and disgustingly decrepit. There was something incredibly wrong about it all, and something in every fibre of my being was screaming it was a rogue, a beast who has taken over its human counterpart. Feral and dangerous.

There was no time for hesitation or thought. I leapt straight off the rooftop, which fell away behind me in an instant. The cold air lashed at my face before my feet slammed so hard onto the stone street I swear I could have easily broken both my ankles, but I was already moving.

The rogue lunged first, coming out of the darkened alleyway like an unforgivable nightmare. Its eyes were wide, red, and bloodshot, with its teeth aimed right for the young prince. I hit the rogue mid-air, and it felt like colliding with a mountain of muscle and fur.

We crashed into the street together with a thud that pushed the wind from my lungs and tormented my ribs instantly.

There was no poise, no grace to my movements, and my hands clawed at the attacker as my jaw snapped wildly and ferociously.

'Shift,' my body and Lex were screaming, but I hadn't even gotten close to perfecting the change, and Lex was also still learning.

Bones began breaking beneath my skin as I half shifted. My arms were lengthening, my fingers snapping into actual claws, canines forcing their way forward, splitting my gums open, and the metallic taste of blood filled my mouth as they did.

Pain exploded through every fibre of my body. But I didn't stop; I couldn't stop. I bit deep into the rogue's flesh, ripping and tearing, still only partially shifted. The rogue was howling as it spun, its claws catching me in the ribs, slicing through the skin as I felt a rib crack from the brutal pressure. But I still couldn't stop!

The rogue outweighed me, but I was faster, meaner, more determined to survive, to live. I bit again and again, and slammed my elbow into the rogue's muzzle as I shoved both of my feet into its stomach, pushing it back. I managed to create enough space between the two of us to swing my arm between us, tearing its throat open under my claws.

Pushing the weight of it off as the blood spilt from its neck, I knelt over the body. The stone around us carrying the blood back down the alleyway from where the rogue came.

The aftermath of the attack was the most alarming. I returned to my normal self as best as I could, claws and canines retracting, Lex calming in my mind. All but the blood, which now covered my body, both mine and the rogue's. Before I could give it much thought, the boots thundered along the alleyway, bringing with them the royal guards in their furs, from victories over the other were-species. I didn't move an inch, just stood there, bloodied, barefoot and starving. Goddess, was I hungry.

Helios, however, moved closer, standing himself right beside me, silent yet confident.

As the king made his way through the guards, his stern eyes fell over the scene.

'One of yours?' he had asked Helios, who only stuttered in response. 'Keep him.' That was it. From that moment on, I was to follow the boy anywhere and everywhere. Helios taught me to stand taller, how to speak properly, and grew up with me. I taught him what pain meant and what loyalty actually was. Somewhere we became more than the Prince and his Stray.

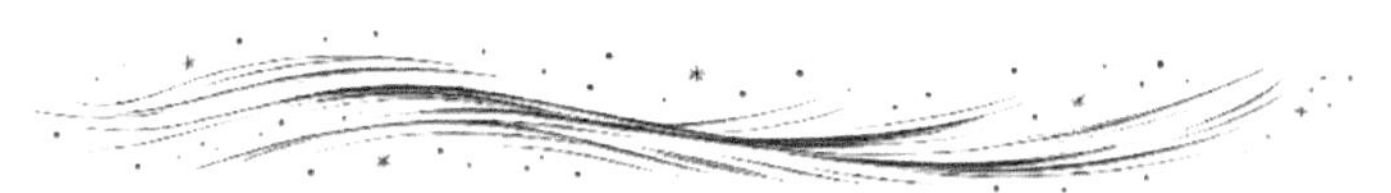

I come back to the Greyfall courtyard slowly, like resurfacing after diving into the depths, and really take in Helios' stance, his balance, the minute adjustments he probably doesn't even realise he's making. I know his stance too well.

His lip twitches. 'You're getting distracted.' He lunges low, and I counter him easily.

'It's been quiet,' I say, breath steady as we circle around again. 'Too quiet.'

'Or peaceful,' Helios shoots back.

I scoff, knocking his arm aside. 'Peace doesn't come after a prince kills his father.'

'You're getting predictable, you know that, right?' I mutter, just loud enough for him to hear, but quietly enough so none of the other fighters in the area could hear me taunting the king.

His lip twitches. Good. It gives me joy to know when I have annoyed him even the smallest amount.

'Careful,' Helios murmurs, voice low and edged, 'you're starting to sound like you need a reminder of why I am the king.' He's never been great at accepting anything less than praise. But that's not what I am here to give him.

Helios shifts, subtle, almost imperceptible to anyone else, but I see it. His weight leans right and his left boot twists just a fraction against the stone.

There it is. He lunges low again.

Anticipating his movements, I'm already moving. I drop with him, catching his momentum before it can rise, forcing his grip higher, my arms instead of my waist, ruining the flow of the strike he thought he'd land on me.

I pivot, turning with him, our boots scraping sharply against the stone. A dance almost. One that has been perfected after many years of learning one and other's instincts as a second nature to our own.

We move together in a synchronised display, our movements growing more ferocious and brutal. The warriors now line the edge of the courtyard, silent and watching through sharp eyes. A lot of these warriors will never get very close to the king, let alone spar against him.

I know every one of them is watching us right now. Watching their Beta and King closely.

Watching for strengths and weaknesses, advantages taken on when to strike and when to defend. Watching and consistently learning. As they are expected to do.

'You say I'm predictable every time we do this, you know?' Helios grunts, while we push back and forth, both grasping onto each other: Helios on my shoulders; me on his forearms, straining against each other.

'And every time,' I say, ducking low to avoid his next swing, 'I'm right.'

He over-committed, again. A terrible idea when he is fighting against me, really. We've partnered in sparring for a long time now; I know his every move. Especially when he wants to show off for those watching, that is when he makes most of his mistakes, and I take every opportunity he has to offer me.

I sweep my leg around, colliding with his and taking them out from underneath him. Helios hits the ground hard enough to make all the surrounding warriors flinch.

I stand over him, tilting my head. 'Dead again, Your Majesty.'

Helios glares up at me, though that infuriating grin is still there. 'Yet, somehow, I am still your king.'

'Momentary lapse, H.' I grin, offering my hand.

It's generally safe to put Helios on his back; it shows the warriors he is just one of us. Both of us trained for many years with the very warriors Helios now commands. He has always insisted that he should not be feared by the men he commands, only by his enemies.

Taking my hand, I haul Helios back to his feet, and his hand heartily claps me on the back, in an open and easy display of our closeness. This isn't Helios, the King. This is Helios, the boy I bled for, the brother I was gifted by the Moon Goddess.

'One of these days, I'm not going to let you win.' He grins at me.

'One of these days, you'll remember how much I enjoy seeing you on the flat of your back.' I reply with an eye roll.

Our laughter booms around the echoing courtyard, cutting through the frosty air. The warriors, who were watching, have recommenced their sparring, hopefully invigorated by our last bout.

Helios rolls his right shoulder, his left hand gripping it as we walk. 'You're slow on your left, Tom,' he comments, wincing slightly with the shoulder movement.

An incredulous snort escapes me. I just put him on his back, but I'm the slow one. 'You happen to be soft through your ribs, Your Majesty.'

Helios' brow raises so high I fear he might lose it in his hairline. 'Careful now, beta. You can still be flogged for insubordination.' His smirk adds to his playful demeanour.

'Do it,' I respond quickly, my voice dry and humourless. 'I could use a little attention.'

Helios barks out a laugh, startling an omega who is walking in the opposite direction. I can't help but smile. He's just ascended to the throne, having had to kill his own father to do it. I am exceptionally happy to see him come back from his own torture.

He hasn't been playful; he has shared no humour, let alone laughter. He has been couped up in his own mind since it happened.

The warmth between us fades quickly as we reach our bags, the wind picking up just enough to stir the hairs on the back of my neck. Enough to raise the hairs on the back of my neck.

The courtyard begins to clear around us as I scull down some water. The training hour has ended, and the warriors are dispersing to get to their duties or to breakfast. Lights are now on down at the homestead, and different sounds of the morning are beginning.

Omega's calling to one and another, horses neighing, their hoofs hammering the ground as they are released from their stalls.

Helios collects his gear, throws his bag over his shoulder just as I do, and starts off toward the archway that leads back to the homestead, and I follow close behind.

'You're quite tense lately, Tom,' he throws back at me over his shoulder as I catch up to walk beside him.

'I think you're seeing things, H.' I shrug.

'No, Tom. I know that look. Something's got you worried,' Helios pressures for more.

'I don't like how quiet things have been,' I admit, watching my own steps. 'You've just taken the crown. Where are the rivals, the challenges that would normally occur when something like this happens with our kind?'

'Maybe no one wants to face off against the King who could kill his own father. No matter how awful that father was as king,' he reasons.

We step out onto the overlook; the rolling hills and green fields spread out to the horizon. Regardless of what he says, I do not trust the quiet or the peace right now. Peace does not equal safety. Just a reason to get complacent, for something worse to come along when it's completely unexpected.

'Something's happened?' I question after watching Helios' face fall in thought.

He doesn't answer immediately, instead, he straightens his spine and works his jaw, like he is chewing on something distasteful.

'What-' I am about to ask when he interrupts.

'A man rode in from the north last night,' he says. 'He claims he was stopped by sentries near the Atticus Star Pack's borders. Half of those he was travelling with were taken.'

I instantly freeze, 'Taken?' I repeat questioningly, making sure I haven't misheard him.

'One of them was his daughter. An omega. Young and unmated,' Helios continues.

'Fucking hell.'

Helios glances at me. 'Language.'

'Really,' I reply, my brow raised.

A very small, knowing smile being all the response I get. I look out over our little slice of peace again, my hands clenching tight around the shoulder strap of my bag.

'Do you think Atticus Star is still running those blood rituals and rites?' I question delicately.

'Unfortunately, I don't have any insiders in the north. But yes, I do.' He runs his hand through his hair, a gesture he does when either frustrated or unsure.

'You know what they are going to do to that poor omega.' The rituals are steeped in the Atticus Star Pack's history. They were torturous and downright inhumane. To this day, they still apparently believe the Moon Goddess wants blood sacrifices of virgins, but only female virgins.

'I know,' Helios' voice is low now. Regretful.

Lex stirs uncomfortably in my mind, not growling, but I can feel the pressure of his emotion combining with mine. A tension building between the two of us that is causing my muscles to continue their ache after our training session.

'They need to be stopped,' I state the obvious out loud. 'We stopped your tyrant of a father. We need to do something in the north as soon as we can. We cannot let this continue.'

'We will-' Helios starts.

'When?' I question instantly.

'When I can do it without starting a war, that's going to burn half of my territory to cinders.' Helios explains.

Turning to fully face him, I sigh. 'Sometimes, I think we need to handle the burn, Helios.'

He looks at me. Really looks at me. It's not in my nature to be so pushy, especially against my closest friend, especially not against the king. But he also needs guidance, and a Beta's job is to guide their alpha, or in my case, the king.

Thankfully, he is well aware I mean him no disrespect and never have. He sees my input for what it is: the truth. But I also understand that he does not want his people to bleed; they have bled enough under his father, but I know he will do it if it means the right justice will be found throughout the entire realm. Not just one section.

'We're not ready yet,' he says after a minute. 'But we will be. You know this. You know we are watching the north.'

My jaw aches from how tightly I've clenched it while we speak, and I nod once. I do understand, but every new piece of information eats at me deeper and deeper. I'm sure it also eats at Helios just as much.

We start walking again, heading back to the homestead. The wind changes again, and immediately a scent catches my senses, causing me to still once more, startling Helios. He stops short, brow arching in that way that means *'Explain'*. The wind is carrying the scent straight through me; it feels like something soft, strange, and comforting. Something floral on the breeze that shouldn't be here. Not the usual scent of the forest surrounding our home, or the dirt of the fields. Something sweeter and far too out of place.

Peonies, perhaps. It's so faint and I would give anything to get the scent from the source.

I feel Lex at attention, hoping for another whiff, his adrenaline surging with mine. I turn my head left and right, sniffing intensely through the breeze, trying with all my might to track it. Which way is it coming from?

'What is it?' Helios asks, having watched my reactions closely. But I don't answer. My pulse has quickened, and I can feel Lex pushing for release. It feels as though something is coming with the wind. Or someone.

And it is calling to me.

Chapter Two

TOM

I LOUNGE IN THE corner chair of my new quarters, one foot braced on the armrest, the other lazily hanging over the same armrest. It's nearly midnight and my glass of scotch is half finished; it burns all the way down, but I barely taste it anymore.

The room smells both dusty and of paper. I reach over, dragging a finger through the dust coating the side table. It comes away grey. The previous beta clearly preferred books to cleaning.

Stacks of them still crowd the room, spines cracked, pages yellowing, left exactly as they were the day he was thrown out. I nudge one aside with my boot just to make space; the clutter is already getting under my skin. I detest hoarders.

We have been moved into the homestead for the past two weeks, but it is quite difficult to get your own areas in working order when the rest of the realm has needed both Helios and me instead.

A fire is glowing from the hearth behind me, heat brushing against the back of my chair while casting flickering lights against the walls. I tip my head slightly, catching my reflection in the darkened window, distorted and unfamiliar in a room that's apparently meant to be mine. Safe and private.

Helios stands at the arched window, his arms folded tightly across his chest, while his gaze never strays away from the northern border so far out past the horizon. His shoulders are stiff, and a muscle in his jaw ticks rhythmically. He's been like this for a while now, worry and anticipation carved into his face, the soft afternoon light as the sun goes down doing very little to sway his attention.

'You feel it, don't you?' he says with no preamble.

I nod slowly. 'Something is shifting. We need to be prepared.'

The silence stretches between us, and the world seems to quiet down around us as even the bird songs fade into the night.

The air feels as though it is wound so tight that the realm is holding its breath, waiting for the next big event to occur.

'The north is stirring,' Helios mutters. 'I hear the whispers. The way the packs all want to continue in the old ways. Especially Atticus Star, their reports are just getting darker. Disappearances have increased, and I know we are the ones who need to do something about it.'

I lean my head back against the chair and take another mouthful of the scotch. 'Then we really do need to cut out the rot before it continues to spread throughout any of the other packs who are thinking, or who are starting to think, the same way as the Atticus Pack.'

Helios turns, his face unreadable. He has a stillness to him I only see when he is thinking more about his failures than any kind of strategy.

The type that shows he is consistently concerned with how he must wait before acting and how many innocents are being put through hell because he is not ready to go to war yet.

When his father lived, terror was all his people knew; it was how he reigned over them all. Helios is trying to be better than his father, trying to be the king the realm deserved all along.

'I should have been ready to act sooner,' he admits. 'I have let too much pass while I have been organising my takeover. I should have taken the crown sooner and acted as quickly as I could once I had. Instead, I waited one, maybe two years longer than I needed.'

'We were surviving, H. Working it all out,' I reply. 'Now we have a real chance to fight and change the way things are done.'

Helios breathes out slowly, and his fingers drag across the windowsill before he moves back toward the desk, sitting in the middle of my room, again laden with heavy books.

His movements are tight and controlled. Like he is trying to stop himself from pacing the length of the room over and over again.

'I miss when our biggest concern was learning how to fight in the compacted dirt training facility where it actually hurt when you hit the ground,' he states, his voice soft.

I smirk into my glass. 'You cried the first time I laid a hit on you.'

He shoots me a look. 'I was twelve!'

'And you cried.'

'That was your elbow. You literally broke my nose.'

'Still counts. You cried.'

A small smile tugs at the corners of his mouth, and the tension that has been filling the room dips for a moment.

A loud knock on the door shatters the quiet within the room.

Helios' head snaps up from the desk, and I push up out of my chair. The door creaks as I open it and welcome one of the young warriors into the room. His eyes are wide, his breath coming in fast, like he has sprinted to find us. His scent hits me before his words do: adrenaline and urgency, sweat covering him and a hint of fear.

'Your Majesty,' he asserts, voice clipped. 'My apologies for the interruption.'

Helios waves him further into the room. 'Speak up.'

'A message from the Greyfall border sentries,' the young warrior says. 'A lone rogue crossed into the outer forest. Fast. Unusually fast. Slipped past the outer team. They are in pursuit, but...' he hesitates. 'They are requesting backup.'

It's interesting to watch the dynamic from the warriors who served beneath his father. This one would have been punished, or worse, for intruding on the previous king. Helios would never consider punishing a man for bringing such important news.

Helios is already moving, crossing the room to follow the warrior.

I set my glass down and roll my shoulders out. *Finally. A chance to stretch.*

We are out the door a second later. The halls are quiet as we pass through them. The scent of ash and pine follows us from the fireplace, but it isn't enough to hide the metallic undertones in the air. Something about this is wrong. We've had many rogues, but this feels different. Lex can feel it too, pacing sullenly just under the surface within my mind. Not tense, exactly, but expectant.

'Do we know anything more about the rogue?' I ask as we pass through the outer gate at speed.

'Nothing more, Beta,' the warrior relays. 'It evaded the sentries, and it moved so fast that the patrol said they barely saw it.'

'Not feral, then,' I grunted.

'No. Completely controlled,' he replies.

That is worse. Feral rogues are violent and tragic. Controlled rogues, they are deliberate. Generally, they have tactics and unknown purposes or intents.

The forest opens up, branches bare above us, and the earth frozen beneath our boots. We move fast through the woods; I, keeping half a pace behind Helios out of habit. The wind shifts slightly, and I stop completely still. The scent, the same one from earlier today, it hits me and my heart stutters. Not the metallic tang of blood, or rot or smoke, or wet fur that is known to be associated with rogues.

Peonies.

Faint and incredibly out of place, wrapped up in something that brings me a feeling of warmth, spreading through my chest as I breathe it in. A scent that seems to be alive and bringing me to life the more I am surrounded by it.

A tremor runs through my body, which has Lex urging me to move, a low growl curling through my chest.

'What is it?' Helios asks, his eyes flicking toward me, slowing his pace.

I stay silent. I can't answer him as it is. I don't know what it is. The scent hits me again—and this time, I move.

Branches scrape against my arms as I push forward, catching on my shirt, clawing at me like they're trying to drag me back. I can barely feel it. My boots skid against loose earth as I change direction sharply, chasing it before it can disappear again.

Lex is already moving in my mind, the adrenaline surging through my veins, pushing me to follow it.

'I'm taking the east flank,' I yell, already turning again with the scent.

'Tom-' I hear Helios begin, but I am sprinting.

'She's not going to wait,' I throw the words back to him over my shoulder without fully understanding them, and I feel Helios completely still behind me. I know he's felt it too, not the mystery scent, but me. My tone, my urgency, my need to get to her. I rake myself through the trees, my feet silent on the frozen ground, wind tearing at my face and heart pounding with every step.

Lex's howl pierces within me, echoing in my ears. The scent is getting stronger and stronger. Someone is calling to us, and goddess help anyone who gets in my way.

The Greyfall forest has always felt alive, and right now, the old trees are looming like sentries, thick-trunked pines and pale birch, their limbs tangled together. Moss grows in thick patches over the stones that litter the forest floor, just as much as it does over the bare, compacted dirt.

I've run through these woods over a hundred times.

But never like this.

My senses are going wild. Thrumming in my ears. Every heartbeat, every crack of bark beneath my boot, every flicker of light being let through the thick canopy. It's all hitting me much harder than it should be. I shove through a low-hanging branch; it snaps back against my shoulder, but I'm already moving again. Faster now, but less controlled.

My claws itch beneath my skin. Lex is pushing for control, to take over and run the forest himself.

I toss a look over my shoulder. Helios is trailing behind, having sent the other sentries to the west flank. 'Try not to fall behind, old boy.'

Helios snorts, I know he is faster than me; he is hanging back out of respect. Knowing this, I grin and push myself harder, stretching out my stride as the trees continue to blur past me. The air tastes like pine as it flashes by before me in the frosty evening.

I crest a rise and the scent of other wolves hits me, the sentries, with nervous and fast beating hearts. I move down to them, gathered by the frozen riverside. Mark is out front, young, sharp, and with wide eyes.

'We tried to flank it,' he says as soon as he sees us. 'But it, it moved like it knows the forest. Like it's reading the terrain as well as any of us who were brought up here.'

Helios steps forward, calm but focused. 'Where did you last see it?'

Mark points to the break in the brush. 'There. It wasn't feral. No blood. No trail.'

My brow pulled together tightly. 'No scent?'

'Not one any of us can follow.'

That doesn't sit right. Nothing alive moved through Greyfall without leaving something behind. Lex stilled in my chest. Then it hits again, carried on the wind. Sun-warmed, honeyed wild peonies. I turn too fast, boots slipping on loose dirt as I try to catch it before it fades. It's stronger this time, closer. Time seems to stand still as the scent wraps itself around me.

My breath catches, and Lex lets loose inside my mind. I stagger, my footing slipping again as the ground tilts beneath me. My hand shoots out, catching against the rough bark of a tree before I can go down completely as the world swims for a moment.

The scent hits again. Stronger. This isn't right.

*No—no, don't—*My knees feel weak and the earth not feeling solid anymore.

This isn't just a scent. It is home, and it shouldn't be out here.

Helios steps closer. 'Tom.'

'I have to follow it.' My voice comes out raw and emotional.

'Wait-'

'I have to.'

'Follow what?' Helios asks.

Lex is now clawing at me internally, demanding we move and now. My muscles are tight and ready to run. The scent is fading, just enough to make the panic rise through Lex and me. She's leaving. She doesn't even know she is mine, and she is already making her way out, leaving me.

Helios reads it on me immediately. The tension in my stance, the low pitch of my responses, and he doesn't argue.

'Go,' he says once again.

I nod once, grateful but shaken, and I run. Faster than I have in a very long time. Faster than I was to bring me to that riverside. The wind is roaring in my ears, and I drop down the ledges, my boots skimming over stones and dirt alike.

Branches whip across my face as I push through them, too fast, too reckless, the scent pulling me like a hook through my chest. Lex surges forward in my mind, sharp and insistent. Not just pacing, driving, urging me while everything narrows to our combined instincts. I don't question it; I am no longer following sounds; I'm not searching for any hidden tracks; I am purely following the ache. The scent. The need.

It pulls me deeper into the woods. Down into the shadows between the trees where the snow is clinging heavily to the ground.

Then I see her. Not clearly, just flashes of her. A shape darting between the trees in a blur of movement. She moves gracefully. Her scent is overwhelming now, sharp to my senses.

Lex growls so loudly that he shakes my core. We crest the slope, and there she is.

Sentries have caught onto her and have her pinned to the snow-covered ground. Two of them, struggling to hold her: one with his arm locked firmly around her middle, the other trying desperately to grasp her wrists as she twists beneath them like fury itself.

And goddess is she fighting. Not wild or reckless. Trained. Every movement I observe is efficient and brutal. She lands a knee to one of their guts, an elbow to the other's jaw. Her shirt is torn down one side. Her arm is bleeding freely from a large slash along it, painting the snow below her bright red, and her mouth is curled up in a snarl sharp enough to be lethal. But why isn't she shifting? Why isn't she letting her wolf protect her?

My body moves before my brain catches up. In an instant, I am airborne, teeth bared, and I slam into the closest sentry, sending him sprawling. The second barely has time to turn before I grab his collar and launch him away from her. Both men hit the ground hard with disgustingly painful sounding thuds.

I am standing between her and them, her and the world, my chest heaving as my eyes lock onto hers for the first time, and everything stops for me.

Hazel. Her eyes are hazel with mesmerising gold, and green flecks which intertwine with the dark. They are wild, terrified, and burning with rage as the bond snaps into place between us, like lightning shooting through my spine. Painful but perfect. Lex roars through me as it takes hold.

I feel it hit her too; her whole body jerks in front of me. Her eyes widen but never leave mine. Her lips part slightly, the shock written all over her. She didn't expect to be running into her mate today.

She blinks; it is as though we are both caught in slow motion, suspended in the current scene playing out between us. I can't breathe and the only thing I can hear is my heartbeat. No, her heartbeat. Our heartbeats.

'Don't,' she whispers, hoarse and broken. Confusion threads through me as I watch her turn from below me and bolt.

Away. She is running from me.

Or at least she tries to. A blur of black intercepts her with ease and stops her instantly.

Helios.

He moves like a ghost, catching her by the wrist, firm but not cruel. She twists in his hand, snarling up at him, her eyes bright and panicked as they flick back and forth from his face to his hand gripping her.

Without thinking, every part of me reacts. I lunge again, this time directly at Helios, growling low as I shove myself between them, baring my teeth and forcing him away from her.

'Let her go,' I demand.

Helios doesn't flinch but releases her wrist instantly. 'She was fleeing. I didn't hurt her, Tom,' he says with a slight snarl. I don't move, my body acting as a wall of protection around her. Lex is huffing, tense and stressed within me. I know Helios is seeing him flashing within my eyes, his possessiveness aching within me, threatening to tear through anyone who gets too close, even our best friend. The same as I am seeing Lucifer now and then as Helios' temper flares as well.

Helios watches me carefully, his eyes analysing every micro movement on my face, the tension that's wracking every muscle, and the auras swirling against each other: beta vs alpha.

'She's your mate, then?' he asks after a beat.

I can't speak; I just nod once. Rough and final.

His eyes shift, understanding perhaps.

'Then she is under your protection,' he says, finality in his voice.

She doesn't move behind me. Doesn't flee again. But I can feel the tremble that is coursing through her, through our bond. Her wolf is strong but unstable, unreachable even. She is definitely terrified of something. I risk a glance back at her; goddess, she is thin. Her lips are parted, her shallow breath visible in the frosty air. She has dirt and blood all over her, which enrages me as I think of the sentries on top of her. Her stunning eyes are still wide, questioning, and very much locked onto mine. She is mine. But it is very clear she doesn't know what to do with that right now. Truth be told, neither do I.

Lex presses into me more. *I want to meet her, Tom.*

I know. So do I. I think we might need patience.

She's terrified. She needs her mate; Lex pushes gently.

I take a slow and grounding breath; everything I had in life has changed within less than an hour. I find calm within myself, slowing my heartbeat and relaxing my muscles and joints. I find the control I need; I can't just touch her.

Not yet.

It is too evident that she is running from something, and whatever it is has her completely terrified. So much so that even our mate bond does not elicit any joy from her. Instead, I just stand here, shielding her from the world with everything I am.

Helios' voice drifts into my mind, breaking the silent panic between us.

We will walk her home.

'Sentries, you can return to your duties. Alert the rest.' He states aloud, breaking the silence in the air.

Chapter Three

THE ROGUE

THE WALK BACK IS slow. Too slow. And exceptionally tense.

Every step they take carries a heavy weight and uncertainty for me. My shoulders stay tight, never quite loosening, no matter how far we go. I absolutely despise uncertainty.

The silence between us all stretches; they don't appear to be very chatty. I despise that almost as much. You can't gather information from silence.

He won't even let me walk. I am being carried like I am the most precious jewel he has ever seen. I say nothing and instead remain still and alert in his arms with my jaw locked tight and my muscles aching from how long they have been straining and taut. My body is trembling, but it has nothing to do with being cold; the heat of my newfound mate bond is radiating between the two of us, pulsing low in my spine and threading through my veins like wildfire.

I have never felt anything so unpredictable, alluring, and so against everything that I am trying to achieve. I need to put as much distance as possible between myself and Atticus Star. I need to regroup, find others who will believe me, and return with as much muscle behind me as possible to save the others.

I don't speak at all while we move through the forest. I don't think I could trust any words that could possibly fall out of my mouth with the mate bond now in place. Anything I say could very well be a muddle of mate bond driven remarks that lead me into a worse predicament than I already am. I can't have that. If I knew his name and this pack, I would have rejected him on the spot.

The forest deepens around us, shadows lengthening as the sun dips behind the cliffs. The trees whispering in the light breeze, causing goosebumps to grace my skin. I am not dressed for the frosty weather; when I ran, I had very little to take with me. I'm not sure if he feels my discomfort or sees the goosebumps, but his arms tighten around me, pulling me closer into his chest, sharing his warmth. My ears catch all the sounds: the men's boots crunching on the frostbitten ground, the rustle of the low-hanging branches as they connect with their shoulders. Even my breath, and his, as it warms the top of my head as he walks in silence, perhaps just as stunned as I am at what has occurred.

I memorise everything. The trails they take me down that are winding and long, the routes, the spacing between the trees as they get wider when the forest thins out, and how long it takes before the packhouse comes into view, or homestead. It's a very odd-looking packhouse. Most packhouses are large, mansion type buildings, homes that exude power and affluence.

This is nothing like them though, more laid back, almost like a farm lifestyle. But if I am to escape, I need to know these things.

My ribs throb with every heartbeat. I was counting those too. My mate remains stoic. But his hold hasn't faltered, not too tight, not overly possessive. His arms are strong and gentle around me, like he is shielding me from the world, and it is... strange.

No one has ever touched me without some form of demand before; no one has touched me without something waiting behind their eyes, generally something sinister.

The bond digs in deeper, and I tense against it automatically, waiting for the threat. For the instinct to push back. But it doesn't come. Instead, my shoulders ease as it feels more like gravity, pulling me directly to him, not just physically but emotionally, and I hate that it doesn't feel like some type of threat to me.

I've heard that mate bonds open up the two people to each other's thoughts and feelings, but for this to occur, the marking has to take place.

My heart skips as we get closer to the homestead. It's too beautiful. But there are no walls. No perimeter fence. No guards posted, at least none I can see. Just open land stretching right up to the buildings, as if nothing out there could ever be a threat.

It's exposed. Too open and too vulnerable.

My jaw tightens and my shoulders stiffen as we step through the door, as I mentally prepare myself for the weight of a collar to grace my neck, or the sting of a blow for the trouble I have caused them all. To kneel, even kiss the boots of those who *saved* me.

But no one reaches for me. No one looks at me as though I am nothing more than a spec of dirt on their foot. Instead, curious glances meet my eyes from many walking through the house, going about their duties. Looks of genuine concern and interest, not the immediate hate and distrust I have grown so used to seeing.

My mate carries me through the main foyer without slowing, the other wolf by his side. People part and bow as he walks, and I can't make heads or tails of them. Why do they bow to them? Not even Aston, the Alpha of the Atticus Star Pack, was ever bowed to by anyone except, of course, those below him who had been taught to never look him in the eye. But those who lived with him in the packhouse never bowed to Aston.

A hallway separates us and the other wolf as he turns down a different one, leaving us together, but the one we take leads us to a quiet wing which is lined with thick rugs and a lot of empty spaces. It looks as though someone has filtered through this packhouse and removed nearly everything that once lived here. The scent of pine and stone surrounds me, and there is a change in pressure in this place. No one here is having to fight for survival daily.

The room we finally enter is private and massive. I can't believe my eyes as I take it all in. Furs layer the bed while the fireplace hisses in the corner as a log drops slightly from the others. The walls are that of dark wood and stone, lined with some books and empty spaces. This isn't the holding cell I was expecting; it's a guest room.

My body tenses as he sets me down gently on the edge of the bed. He doesn't linger over me or touch me again, even though my body now feels empty without his hands and chest warming me. He doesn't actually press for anything, nothing that I can feel the mate bond is calling for, no questions about where I came from or what I am doing running through their territory. Nothing.

'My name is Tom,' he says, his eyes never leaving mine. 'I am the Beta of the Lycan pack of Greyfall. You are my mate, and I am going to take care of you. The other wolf you met is Helios. He is my closest friend and the Lycan King over the territories. He will help us sort this all out.' He's speaking to me like I am a wounded animal. I guess I *am* a wounded animal.

My fingers curl in the soft blanket under me, all the kindness feels something of a trick. Almost like I am waiting for the other shoe to drop, and to be brought to the actual cells for my indoctrination into this pack.

Tom answers a small knock on the door almost instantly, and a small omega enters, carrying a tray and a bag slung over her shoulder. She moves around Tom, into the room with ease, giving a small head bow to him, which he returns. She moves directly to me, kneeling, but when she lifts her head, her eyes meet mine, steady and assessing rather than lowered.

'This is May. She is one of our best healers in the pack. I would like her to check you over if you will allow it,' Tom explains.

I nod slightly, still watching this omega.

She doesn't hover at the edges like most would. Instead, she steps fully into the space, meeting Tom's presence head-on. No flinching, no hesitation, just quiet certainty.

And Tom… he doesn't correct her. Doesn't dismiss her. He *trusts* her.

As soon as May picks up on my acceptance, she begins examining me, her eyes sharply darting along my arms and her gentle hands pressing and feeling poorly mended bones and the latest half healed beatings.

'This might sting,' May murmurs, not to Tom, but to me. 'Tell me if it's too much.' She applies ointment to the injury I received during my tussle with the guards tonight; she has picked up on my delayed healing. The wolfsbane in my veins prevents any care my wolf would normally provide. The entire time I can't relax. I keep my eyes down, not wanting to see Tom while my punishment for my last act of defiance is shown.

'She is dehydrated, Beta,' May tells him, her voice low. It's now that I look at him and see him turn around to watch us. He has not been watching us the entire time, instead offering us privacy while my wounds from tonight and before were examined.

'Malnourished. Multiple healed fractures, albeit poorly... some within the last month. Bruising under the ribs.' May pulls her satchel over her shoulder. 'But no infections. I will need to tend to the most recent injuries from this evening again in the morning. But she greatly needs rest, food, and water.' She takes a hesitant breath, flashing Tom a look. 'There is wolfsbane in her blood. It could take up to a week before her body can process it out, depending on how long it has been getting pushed into her.' She finished with a sigh.

I stare at the far wall while she discusses the damages with him. He's the beta of this pack, no wonder they bowed. I'm fated to one of the highest ranked members of this Greyfall pack. Of course, he is. Of course, this is my luck. Forced toward an atrocious alpha and fated to a beta I don't even know.

Tom stands silently, listening to May. His eyes darting between me and her, every injury she mentions, his eyes flick to that part of me. His arms are crossed firmly across his chest, his body is tense, and I can feel the frustration and anger burning within him through the bond. Even though his external composure shows no sign of it.

He is fighting the bond. I can feel him. It is calling for the gap between us to be closed. It's calling to him just as much as it is calling to me to fulfill it. The instinct to mark and claim one another, to settle the tension I feel within it between us.

But he simply thanks the omega as she leaves and stands by the door, watching me like I am a piece of some puzzle he doesn't understand. Another knock, and Helios enters not long after the omega has left. The aura I feel without panic clouding my senses is undeniable; there is no room to assume he would be anything but the Lycan King, as Tom said.

He doesn't speak right away. Instead, he stands by Tom, his eyes flashing between gold and darkness and cloudiness, discussions with his wolf. Tom's eyes then go cloudy. I have seen this before: two members linked through their minds. They can have an entire discussion about me, in front of me, without me ever knowing what words were spoken. It's happened many times before.

'Who is she?' Helios finally asks aloud, his voice flat.

'She hasn't given a name yet and I haven't pressed,' Tom answers carefully.

'But you brought here. Protected her from your own men, some which have now received medical care.' Helios' eyes flick between the two of us.

'She's my mate. You said it yourself.' The words thicken the air between us all.

Helios looks at me, really looks at me, and my throat goes dry, constricting.

'Are you certain?' Helios asks.

Tom doesn't hesitate. 'Both me and Lex are certain. This isn't something you can get wrong, H.'

Helios sighs, slow and deliberate, turning slightly more toward Tom. 'Then, this is going to get complicated. We know she has come down from Atticus Star.' I go still. My fingers curl into my palms, nails biting just enough to ground me. Heat rises along my ears, and I force my breathing to stay even, slow in, slow out, like nothing's wrong. My eyes sting. I blink hard, but I can't stop the thought of being taken back, feeling fear tightening in my chest.

Tom's jaw flexes, protection lacing through our bond instantly as he picks up on my distress. 'I don't care; manage it.'

'You will care,' Helios' voice, though softer now, is extremely measured. 'The council will want-'

'I don't care what the council will want, Helios. They can go to the gods below,' Tom snarls, turning to Helios.

I flinch from the bed. My hands are curling tighter and tighter into the fur. Although my body is still, the words are ringing in my chest like a physical blow while my need to get out of this place is growing by the second. The need to put more distance between me and Aston is growing fast in my mind. The council, politics.

I'm not a mate, and what a joke to think I am; I'm a problem. Even here and now, a new pack. Even with a bond forged between me and the Beta, the two of them speak of consequences, councils, and appeasing a terrible pack alpha like Aston.

'I can reject-' I begin, but Tom shoots me a look that I have never seen accompanied with the emotions rushing through our bond before. Anger, not at me, but his alpha, and terror that I would break our fated bond.

'Don't. Don't finish that sentence,' he growls out, his eyes boring into mine. Tom immediately stalks to the bedside. 'I would not accept it. So, I beg you, do not put yourself through that,' he finishes softer, lifting the furs and gesturing for me to slide fully underneath them.

'We can discuss this at a later time, please.' Tom looks up at Helios, who simply nods and leaves the room.

This is not what I wanted when I ran. I let my eyes fall shut, Tom still by the side of the bed. Watching.

Chapter Four

THE ROGUE

THE ROOM IS QUIET, except for the fire that is crackling and hissing in the corner. The heat, bringing with it the memories of the forest, my mate and the newfound pack, that I am definitely not sure about. Gold and orange lights are dancing along the stone walls and the floor.

I sit curled in the furs, my legs folded beneath me, my spine straight but aching, the tension still haunting my body, keeping me alert and wary.

The cup in my hands is steaming, filled with a healing broth. The salt and herbs turn my stomach every time I sniff them, but the healers are hoping it will not only speed my recovery but also speed up the process of removing the wolfsbane from my body. I have been so long drugged with wolfsbane that I am not sure if my wolf, Sylvie, has even survived.

May presses my hands, tilting them up higher to my lips before rising. 'Drink it,' she commands, not unkindly.

I don't look up, but I hear the soft shift of her steps and the quiet click of the door latch as it closes behind her.

Only Tom remains.

He sits on the floor near the bed, his elbows resting on his knees. His back casually leaning against the post, breathing like he is wound as tightly as I am, like he isn't watching me from the corner of his eye. But he is. He seems to always be watching.

He hasn't said much since we came back from the woods. No questions of me. Just soft remarks here and there. Calm words. Safe ones. He hasn't demanded I talk, and so I guess I probably should.

'I was raised in the Atticus Star Pack,' I say out of the blue, causing Tom to startle slightly.

His gaze flicks up to me, but he doesn't interject.

'They train you early,' I continue. 'You learn submission before you even learn how to shift. You're broken down long before you could even possibly understand what freedom is or looks like. You are taught to be silent and obedient. That you're disposable.' I try to keep the bitterness from my voice, trying to remain as stoic as he is, but it's difficult and I am incapable of it.

I remember the training pits they would force us all into. The scent of blood was so strong there that it would stay with you for days. And the instructor's hand, pressing down on my neck until my knees would give way. A shudder runs through my body at the thought of the force.

'I wasn't very good at it. Submission or obedience.' The corner of my mouth lifts, not in a smile, more like a twitch. 'I fought back against the current status quo. Back talked to all those who would try to think themselves owners of us all. Took punishments that weren't meant for me, because some of the younger omegas wouldn't have been able to recover from yet another bruise. For a while, they let me.' I shift the cup between my palms. 'Thought I'd outgrow it, or that they could beat it out of me.' I still feel some bruises years later. Phantom pains beneath the skin.

Tom's jaw flexes slightly as I talk.

'When I first shifted,' I continue, not sure if I should, but Tom seems safe; I can't help but want to tell him everything. Maybe this is what the bond does to people: share absolutely everything between them. 'They realised I wasn't going to bend. My wolf, Sylvie, she's fierce. We were faster, meaner, and we wouldn't kneel. They didn't like that,' my voice drops to a whisper. 'So, they did the only thing they could do. They locked me in one of the houses reserved for training disobedient females. Those who fight back are always corrected, and harshly. They filled me with wolfsbane weekly. Without Sylvie, I couldn't heal properly, couldn't fight back as hard. I was kept in isolation. No running, no moonlight. Just me, a collar and walls.'

I stare into the fire, willing it to take away the memories.

'They told me I would be the alpha's next Luna. But I had to learn to be quiet enough. Pretty enough. Obedient enough.' The memories bring back the scent of the room they kept me in, musty and metallic. 'I didn't break; I couldn't.' I say flatly. 'So, they tried desperately to destroy me instead. Making sure they performed their duties to make me the perfect Luna for the Alpha. Weekly beatings became daily; more wolfsbane, less humane captors.'

I grip the cup tighter as it shakes in my now trembling hands. Tom remains silent, but the shift in him is sharp. Like his skin isn't fitting right, like the wolf I can sense within him is pacing just beneath his ribs, in his mind and wants out.

'I ran when the Luna died. I had to. During the mourning rites. They were all distracted; I slipped out, hoping they would never catch me.' My throat burns with emotion as the words fall out. 'I guess I made the mistake of coming too close to your territory; your guards are very sharp. Much better than those who let me slip out of Atticus.'

I turn to Tom and, for the first time; I meet his gaze straight on. His eyes are storm colours, focused and unshakable.

'I didn't run because I was afraid.' I say, my voice drifting off.

The fire hisses as a log split down the centre, sparks spitting out.

Tom breathes out slowly. 'And now?' he asks. His voice is steady, but I can hear the strain in it.

I set the cup aside. 'I need to go back.'

He doesn't flinch at my words.

'Not to beg or kneel,' I say. 'I want to burn that pack to the ground. I want to see the omega collars shattered and the cells empty. I want the ones still trapped there to know what freedom feels like, and I want to give it to them.' My voice cracks, rage filling my body.

The rage that becomes something short of holy retribution.

I look at my hands, some marks still healing across my fingers. A faint shadow of the old scar where wolfsbane had been pressed against my wrists for days on end without food or reprieve.

'I used to believe surviving meant I still have something left to offer. That if I was breathing, I hadn't lost yet. But lately…'

My throat tightens around the words. 'Lately, it feels like surviving is a different type of defeat.'

Silence grew comfortably between us, like we have known each other our whole lives, perhaps our intertwined souls have.

Tom shifts, then stands. He moves slowly and deliberately. He still doesn't touch me, doesn't even reach out, but he kneels beside the bed, one of his hands resting lightly on his thigh, the other hovering lightly in the space between us. Open and waiting.

I stare at his palm, the small scar across his thumb, and the way his fingers curl just slightly. He's steady, but not passive. I have felt Sylvie getting strong while we have been here, and it's a blessing from the Moon Goddess to feel her now, pressuring me to him. Not with desire, but with recognition of a kindred spirit. Someone who will protect us from the things that lurk within the shadows, and for the first time in years, something inside me eases. Just enough.

I place my hand in his, and he simply curls his fingers around mine. No pressure or demands, just a reassurance of his presence.

'What's your name?' he asks gently as his hand warms mine.

Chapter Five

KIRA

'KIRA,' I SAY QUIETLY, almost scared to let him know. But the fire in his eyes burns brightly, and he smiles softly as though my name is the most beautiful thing he has ever heard in the world.

Tom doesn't promise me revenge. He hasn't vowed to bring my enemies to their knees in bloodshed or war or any kind of retribution.

'You're safe,' is the first thing he says to me. 'While you're here, no one will touch you. No one will question you.' And somehow, his words land much harder for me than any promise of violence and revenge ever could have. I wait for the rest of it. The part where he tells me what the cost is. But my worth to Tom doesn't appear to have conditions. He hasn't said that I am safe because I am his or because he is here to protect me because of the mate bond we share. He just said I was safe to exist, and no one has ever given me that without wanting something in return. Something lessens in my chest.

I don't thank him; I don't even know where I would begin or how to.

I swallow, my throat tight, my fingers curling around his before I can second-guess myself. His skin is warm and welcoming under mine.

'Don't go,' I whisper, and the words scrape on the way out. It isn't pride that stops me from saying more; it's fear.

Fear that if I ask for too much, he'll see how desperately I need this, need him, and decide I am too broken to keep.

'Just… stay, please. With me.' My voice trembles despite my efforts to steady it.

Tom takes up the chair across the room, the one near the window, and pulls it close enough that he can see the door by the bedside. Typical protector move, I assume. But he doesn't sit on the edge like a guard would, no. Instead, he leans back slowly, his long legs stretching toward the fireplace, and arms resting on the wide armrests like he's been here a million times before. Like this was something as normal as the blue in the sky. Like I am not broken. I lie still for quite some time, pretending to sleep, watching him from the sliver of an eye.

He still doesn't move or speak. His breathing is slow and syncing with the rhythm of the fireplace, almost.

My eyes burn. I blink once, twice, and I drift. I don't dream, at least not that I remember, but I wake in a cold sweat. My fists clenching into the damp furs beneath me, and my breath catching, shallow and quick, like I have been running hard through the forest. My heartbeat hammers against my ribs, hard enough that I press a hand to my chest, half-expecting to feel it bursting outward with every thump.

No chains are on me, no collar. But the room feels smaller, the ceiling pressing lower onto the bed. The walls seeming closer than before. I sit bolt upright, staring into the fireplace as it glows back at me.

Tom is still here, but he doesn't move. His eyes stay fixed on me, steady and unblinking, like he's waiting for me to bolt.

He holds up a small cup of water, his hands steady.

I reach for it, our fingers brushing against each other, and I flinch before I can stop myself. The smallest touch sends the most electric pulse through my entire body. I take the cup and sip, then drain it entirely, tasting none of it.

The water scrapes down my throat, burning the dryness and then easing, leaving a raw coolness behind as I try to regain my ability to swallow, and breathe.

Tom still remains silent, which seems to be a feature of his by this point. He just watches with his storm grey eyes that don't flinch or pity. I turn back to the fire, focusing on the way the wood caves in on itself, glowing, collapsing, anything but the noise in my own head.

'I'm sorry. I still wake up thinking I am still there, even on the nights I was sleeping under the moon. That the walls are closing in on me and I am back in the room having only dreamt of being free.'

'Well, you're not there,' his voice comes out rough, like he hasn't spoken in weeks.

'I know,' I glance at him. 'But my body doesn't understand that yet.'

Tom nods once. He doesn't say anything after that. Doesn't offer suggestions, doesn't try to fill the silence, just stays where he is, watching me like he's waiting for something I haven't decided yet. The fire has burned low and been fed again at some point; I don't remember when. There's an empty cup near his hand; I guess he hasn't left the chair.

When I drift again, it's uneven, restless and cold despite the fire still burning steadily in the corner. I wake to the sound of wood dragging softly against the floor, inching closer to the bed. I don't open my eyes. But I feel the shift in the room. The space between us is smaller now. Almost like he believes that the closer he physically is to me, the easier it will be for me.

I lose track of the day somewhere between one fire and the next. Light crawls across the floor, disappears, then returns again.

I don't get to heal magically. Not like other were-people. Not with a bath and a meal and a few hours for the sinew, muscles, and skin to repair themselves under the guidance of the internal wolf. No, for me, there's no sudden shift. It starts as an itch, deep under my skin, too deep to reach. I drag my nails over my arms, anyway, chasing it, but it only spreads. My nerves spark to life, one by one.

Too sharp.

Too bright.

My body doesn't remember how to hold it all at once.

I curl in on myself, teeth clenched, riding it out.

Then, something loosens as the wolfbane loses its hold over my body and my muscles are able to relax more than they have in months. The tension in the fibres of my body, which were holding me hostage, is dissipating. My shoulders drop, just slightly, and I freeze at the feeling. My jaw unclenches and my hands stop shaking long enough to notice they were.

Slowly, the slow, restless pacing at the edge of my mind grows. My wolf, Sylvie, swirls between us, flickering, but growing stronger and stronger. Her pacing my mind, reconnecting through our thoughts. I knew I missed her terribly, but feeling her in my mind is a completely different and welcome type of freedom for us both.

I press a hand to my chest, like I can anchor her there, like she might slip away if I breathe too hard. And for the first time in longer than I can remember, I am not alone in my own head.

He is handsome and strong. His wolf has a very large presence. I can sense them both. Sylvie is almost instantly enamoured by our mate.

And patient, I add with a little sigh. *It just also feels too good to be true.*

He has brought us back together, Kira. If he gives us nothing else, this is enough. But I don't believe that is all he wishes to give to you.

She is right, and over the next few hours I walk with him through the packhouse, getting to know more about him, his pack, and how I can possibly fit in here.

He pauses for everyone. Listens when they speak, even the young cubs and the omegas. No snapping orders, and no one flinching when he steps close. A warrior claps him on the shoulder as he passes. Someone laughs at something he says. No one lowers their eyes unless they choose to. I find myself watching him longer than I mean to. He is incredibly different from the wolves I have left.

This… is not what I'm used to. He is loved, not feared. Embraced, not flinched at.

Greyfall's corridors open before him without hesitation. Pack members move against the stone walls when he approaches, not out of fear, but habit and, I think, respect. He doesn't slow or quicken; he just continues his stride, steady, with an echo of his boots as they hit the stone.

I stay half a step behind him. Not hidden, but not quite beside him either. No one reaches for me, and no one is weighing or judging me while I am with him.

They notice me and let me be.

Tom's stride never changes; he is steady and confident. I match it without even thinking.

A pair of warriors straighten as he passes. One thumps a fist against his chest.

Tom returns it easily. The other's gaze flicks to me, quick and assessing, but not hostile, just curious.

I brace for the question, but it doesn't come, and we keep moving.

At the stairwell, a guard grins as we approach, stepping forward to clasp his forearm in a firm, practiced grip.

'Shift was quiet?' Tom asks the guard.

'Aye.' A pause between them stretches for a moment. 'Too quiet.'

Tom's eyes sharpen slightly.

Then the guard's gaze shifts to me. Not lingering, just enough to register.

Tom doesn't pause this time.

'This is Kira,' he says, like it's the most natural thing in the world. 'My mate.'

The word lands heavier than it should, and the guard straightens ever so slightly.

'Kira,' he acknowledges me with a small nod.

No disbelief. No challenge. Just acceptance. My throat tightens anyway.

Near the kitchens, an omega struggles with a basket stacked too high with linens. The top bundle slips, and I move before I think. My hand catches the edge, steadying it before it can fall.

The omega startles, eyes flicking up to mine. For a moment, I expect her to pull away. Many would have in Atticus Star, scared to be flogged for their failure of needing help.

'Thank you,' she says, a little breathless. Her gaze flicking between Tom and me before heading off on her duties.

We continue.

No whispers follow us. No tension trails in our wake. Just the steady rhythm of a place that runs because he's part of it, not because it fears him.

He doesn't fill the halls with his voice. He listens. To the murmured complaints, the subtle shifts in tone when someone hesitates before answering. And when he finally gives an instruction, when he speaks, the air tightens, not in fear, but in attention. No one asks him to repeat himself. Which is how I know this isn't a show for me; this is him and his connection to his pack.

When he looks at me, Goddess, when he looks at me, it's never with ownership over me. More like a quiet adoration, like he is admiring something he has wanted his whole life. He watches me like he's trying to memorise something. Like if he looks too fast, I might disappear.

He's brought me all of my meals so far, not a servant or another omega. I think it is so we can eat together; he always brings just enough for the two of us and always warm. He has been respectful, placing the meals within reach of wherever I am sitting, and sitting in comfortable silence together while we eat.

After dinner, Tom hands me a worn book, its edges have been softened with age. 'Southern packs,' he says simply. I guess if I am to stay here, fated to the beta, I should probably know a little about them. I flip through the pages with him while I am curled beneath the blanket, trying to ignore the lingering ache in my ribs, Sylvie has certainly eased the healing process and helped with speeding it up slightly, but I am still getting twinges here and there. Noticing the wince, Tom takes the book from me and begins reading about the Dreamshire Pack, which is written in elegant handwriting, to me.

While listening to him, I try to ignore the growing heat rising in my core. The heat that is becoming too difficult to ignore with every passing interaction with Tom. It coils slowly, tightening and wrapping itself around me, filling me with warmth as the goosebumps spread across my skin as it fills every fibre beneath it.

His presence has softened my edges. His continuous care and dedication over the few days I have been fated to him has brought a different side out of me, one that isn't scared to think about a possibility of a future with this man. I can't help watching him as he sleeps in the armchair, having drifted off a little after reading through the book. His arms are folded loosely over the book, resting on his chest. His chin is tucked slightly, and his hair has fallen across his brow.

I study his hands while I can, the ones that I watched throw trained guards around like they were nothing more than kindling, the hands which lifted me as if I am something worth saving.

As I think of his arms wrapped around me on the walk through the forest, the bond hits me hard, pulling at me, pulsing within me. Like it is growing like a vine between the two of us, trying to tie us together with every passing minute. But I don't quite trust it, or myself perhaps, but I can't very well turn away from it either.

Sleep comes slowly, tangled in my thoughts. I drift in and out of dreams threaded with warmth and doubt, and when dawn finally presses against the window, I feel as though I haven't rested at all.

The next morning, the scent reaches me before I reach the table; where melting butter, sweet pancakes, eggs and bacon fill the plates. My stomach tightens despite everything.

Tom is already seated at the table, sunlight cutting across the table and catching in his hair. The stack of pancakes sits between us, steam curling lazily into the air.

For a moment, neither of us speaks.

He slides the platter of pancakes toward me, his eyes blazing into mine, and his fingers brush mine when I reach for it, brief, accidental. Or perhaps not.

'Eat,' he says quietly.

I tear a piece of pancake free instead of taking a whole one. He notices, his eyes narrowing on my movements. Of course he does. A moment later, he cuts one in half and places it on my plate as though that had been the intention all along. 'Eat more,' he says, shooting me a playful, boyish smile for the first time since we met.

We pass the bacon and eggs back and forth.

The room smells of salt and sugar and strong tea steeping too long in its pot. It feels like something that should be ordinary, something other people experience daily.

But it doesn't. Nothing about this is ordinary for me, yet still, my shoulders loosen, just a fraction, but I keep waiting for something to snap. This entire experience has me rattled and content all in one.

Goddess, it has been a very serious couple of days.

Tom is sitting across from me, completely serious, trying to explain how Helios once mistook a racoon for a scout from another pack. Tom's expression doesn't change once it remains dry, so deadpan serious, that I couldn't stop the laugh from escaping, startling us both. I clamp a hand over my mouth, trying to stifle the noise, but it slips through anyway, completely out of my control.

For the first time in a long time, it's a genuine laugh. Not bitter or hollow, but real. Something I wasn't sure that I would ever feel again. But Goddess, it hurts. My ribs pull, breath catching, and I curl slightly inward, but I'm still laughing.

Tom's mouth twitches, and little by little, he makes me think it might be okay to feel these emotions deeper. To enjoy something the world, mainly my mate, has to offer.

The scent of coffee hangs around Tom, enthralling my senses while we eat, and I feel like he is pulling me into something safe; he's making sure I don't feel like I am a problem. Our knees nearly touch under the table, and I don't move away. For a moment, I forget to brace.

Tom… he makes me feel human.

Chapter Six

TOM

THE CHAIR ACROSS FROM mine scrapes softly against the floor as Kira stands. She reaches for the plates, then stops halfway, glancing at me before following through and gathering up the plates, as though she's done this a hundred times before.

I watch the way she studies the table and how she thinks she is going to manage carrying the used dishes by herself. She doesn't look at me almost as though she already thinks I won't step in; it's clear she's used to doing these types of chores alone. But that isn't her future. I have already signalled to the omegas that we have finished; but she doesn't ask, she just starts doing, like slowing down or stopping might make her unwanted or unneeded. She doesn't realise her only concern right now is to heal.

I stand the moment she realises the knock on the door is going to take care of the dishes. I'm already tracking the shift of her weight, the quiet inhale before she moves away from the table.

She doesn't take three steps without me noticing. Most times, she doesn't take one without me following. Meetings, even the dull obligations I would normally perform by myself, I bring her with me, or I cut them short. It is my absolute mission to make sure she is with me as much as possible.

Nearly a week of this, and still, it isn't enough.

Kira adapts quickly. Watches. Learns. Following the rhythm of the house as though she's always belonged here. Her interactions with the other members, although few, seem natural.

But not quite.

There's hesitation in her, a small, almost unnoticeable stillness. Whether she pauses at a doorway, or she shows a flicker of uncertainty when someone looks at her for a moment too long.

I notice every time.

I hate it, and so does Lex.

She is my mate and she should be completely confident in our connection, that this is her home, that she is welcome and fits in here.

I don't let her stray far. Not until the next morning, when my Beta duties force my attention elsewhere for longer than I like. Her absence leaves an unsettled feeling in the pit of my stomach, much more intensely that I expect it to.

When I track her down, I find her in the corner of the library mid-morning, the sunlight spilling through the windows, highlighting her features like the goddess she is. Just sitting there, staring out the window, a large book resting on the top of her thighs. I close the door behind me, not taking my eyes off her.

Snow falls from my boots with every step I take toward her, leaving a trail of cold in my wake.

Our eyes meet as her face flashes upward, a small smile present, and a stir in our bond as desire for her fills me instantly.

'I spoke with Helios,' I start.

Kira takes a sharp breath and lets it out slowly. Her gaze drops to the floor at the mention of Helios; her shoulders tighten, and she stills. The slight tug in the bond toward her tells me when she is uncomfortable, and her thoughts on our king make her so.

'He agrees. We will head to Atticus Star. On paper, it will be seen as a diplomacy venture. A show of goodwill and strength between our packs with Helios' rise to the crown. But we will watch closely; we will see how much they show us, and how much they hide.'

Kira just sits, staring at me as though she doesn't trust she heard me correctly. 'You would do that?' She asks quietly.

I take the final few steps that separate us. 'I would do anything for you,' I say honestly. 'You said you wanted to go back and fix the issues. I won't take that from you; I will help you achieve the justice you want.'

Kira's eyes widen, and a moment flashes between us. Not exactly understanding, more like acceptance.

'You're not afraid to fight for someone you just met?' Her voice is small; she still doesn't understand how important she truly is to me.

'I am afraid, but not of that,' I counter.

Kira rises from her chair and takes a step closer, her eyes never leaving mine. My control is slipping, her scent is ensnaring my senses. All I want to do is hold her, take her, mark her as mine. Closing the distance completely, Kira's fingers deftly reach up and take hold of the front of my shirt, grabbing the fabric hard and tugging me down slightly. The bond is pulling between us now, harsh and desperate to be completed. Like ash settling in my chest, the heat is tearing through every atom and fibre that makes me, causing my fingers and toes to tingle and my limbs to feel like they are on fire.

Lex is unsettled within me, his possessive snarls echoing through me.

She's mine. Finally.

I swallow my control back as much as I can. This moment between us isn't a hunt or a claim. It is to remain her decision completely.

'What if I don't wish to wait any longer?' Kira asks softly; it's like she is reading me like an open book.

My breath catches hard at her words. The control I've been clinging to slips, heat flooding my veins so fast it leaves me unsteady.

Blood rushes brutally to the south as her words play in my mind, my cock thickening against the material of my pants. I flex my hands at my sides as I step closer to her, just the smallest amount, slow and deliberate, giving her space to pull away if she prefers. But she doesn't.

'I'll follow your lead,' I say, my voice rougher than I meant it to be.

But I mean the words, I will do anything for her. Anything she could ever ask of me.

The kiss takes me completely by surprise. Kira is up on her toes, her lips crashing into mine, hard and desperate with need, like it is our last day together, the last action she would ever take.

Kira's hands fist my shirt, dragging me down to her as she lowers off her toes. The taste of her floods my mouth, sweet with something wild within her. Her scent, the only scent that matters to me, peonies, engulfing my absolute everything.

I groan low; the sound coming out of me as I kiss her back, but slower, deeper, a more grounding connection between us as I slowly take control inch by inch.

Easy, Lex interjects. *Don't rush. Don't frighten her.*

Goddess help me, she is fire itself and I don't think I can frighten her now, even if it was my intent.

Kira pulls back from me. 'Take off your shirt.'

I have never been commanded to do anything by anyone other than Helios since we met. But with her words, my hands instantly move to remove it. I strip it off without breaking eye contact with Kira, letting it fall to the floor. Her gaze tracks every inch of me, her eyes darkening with desire, and the heat of her watchful eyes is causing my skin to tighten with need.

Her fingertips reach out, tracing the old scars that litter my torso. Following the muscles and defined lines like she is learning me completely.

'What are they from?' Her curiosity is understandable. Lycans and Werewolves can usually heal without scars, without time. But wolfsbane, as she would be fully aware, given her previous circumstances, hinders that ability.

I let out a shaky breath beneath her touch; no one has ever made me feel this way. Like something to explore, to enjoy.

'They healed,' is all I can muster, my voice very unlike my usual tone.

I let my hands wander to the hem of her top, stopping gently and watching her closely.

'Yes?' is all I ask of her.

Kira's single nod hits me harder than any command ever could or would. The permission I had never felt I needed to have before now. I pull the fabric up slowly, revealing her beauty little by little. I don't want to rush this. I want to take her in, every single part of her. Her lean strength, the soft swell of her breasts rising and falling with her very unsteady breaths, and her scars. Just like mine.

I look over all of hers, many healed lines and spots, and my eyes shoot up to hers, which are looking almost apologetic at me. As though she deems herself unworthy, scarred and tainted for not being untouched. But I know how she got these scars only too well, and standing in front of me, all I see is perfection.

My mouth feels dry, my fully hardened cock is aching, and she is so beautiful in a way that hurts me deep in my soul. No, she is not untouched, but she is completely mine.

I kiss her again, but this time my tongue slides against hers as my hand maps her back, fingers gliding along her skin, feeling every part of her that makes her perfect, and memorising how she fits against me, in my arms.

We stumble back toward the fireplace at the centre of the back wall, the library books now a blur in the background. I follow her down onto the furs and brace myself above her, refusing to pin her below me. Even as every instinct is screaming at me to cage her below me and sink my canines into her neck.

Instead, I busy my hands with removing my pants and hers. Slowly, gently gliding the material along her legs, letting her feel the softness of the movement and the desire as I greedily take her nakedness in. Repositioning myself above her, her legs part around me without hesitation.

Fuck.

The groan tears from me before I can try to stop it, raw and wanting. My hips rock instinctively, friction sparking between us, and she gasps, soft and just as needy as I feel.

'You feel that,' I murmur against her throat, my teeth grazing her skin, canines aching to be elongated and marking her. Kira nods below me, already breathless. 'That's not fate.' I say quietly. 'That's me wanting you. All of you. Just as you are. Every. Single. Inch.' I kiss her with every word, thrusting slightly, letting her feel what she does to me.

A sharp prick of pain lances through my shoulders as her nails dig into my skin, not a pain I would ever shy away from, but a pain I instead lean into.

'Show me how much you want me.'

That is it; my restraint shatters completely with her words.

I kiss her all over, down her throat, her chest, my mouth needy and hot as I taste her, tease her, enjoying learning the sounds she makes as the pleasure builds inside her. The moans of more when I hit just the right spot on her soft and sensitive skin.

Kira arches beneath me, the sound of a broken moan tearing from her lips. I slide my hand lower, my finger brushing between her thighs. She is already slick with want and need, aching and thrusting herself up to meet the palm of my hand.

I can't help the groan that comes from me as I feel her, warm and ready as she continues bucking into me.

'Tom,' she breathes, my name sounding like heaven on her lips. Hearing my name coming from her in such a breathy way nearly undoes me. Instead, I position myself slowly, deliberately giving her time. Always giving her time to pull away from me if she feels the need.

Kira cries out as I press forward, stretching her inch by careful inch. Her muscles tense beneath me, and I freeze, dropping my forehead to hers and waiting.

'Okay?' I ask gently.

Pressing her is the last thing I want from my mate. I would wait a lifetime for her.

'Yes,' she whispers. 'Please.'

I push inside her fully with a low groan next to her ear. Tight and hot, my goddess given mate is perfection.

Our bond flares up white hot between us, her heartbeat echoing in my pulse as I move slowly, watching her face as the pressure builds within us. Watching her trust me with her body and soul, watching her choose to enjoy our mate bond for the first time since it snapped into place between us.

She meets every thrust eagerly, rocking herself up into me, her breath quickly turning ragged.

The realisation that she is choosing me shatters something deep inside. I pick up my pace, thrusting deep and deliberate into her, the sound of my skin meeting hers filling the room. Her voice breaks as she gasps, calling my name again and again.

I watch as she comes apart beneath me, her whole-body trembling, her eyes shut tight and her mouth open in a silent cry. Seeing her so fulfilled, so beautiful, has me losing control. I drive into her one final time, my release ripping through me as I collapse against her, shaking and panting into her skin.

For a long moment, there is nothing but breath and heat between us as the bond settles back into the uncomfortable, yet still comforting sensation I have grown accustomed to. I won't mark her, even though every part of me and the bond itself is screaming for it. I want to make sure she knows it is more than a physical need for me. When she lets me, when she asks, I will mark her and she, me.

I gather her up carefully in my arms; she is one of the most precious people in my life. I relish the feel of her pressing her face into my neck, the heat of her breath warming my skin.

'I forgot what safe feels like.' She murmurs to me.

My chest tightens as she speaks, and for the first time since this fate has found me, I know with terrifying certainty that I will burn the world down for this woman. She will never know what unsafe feels like from now.

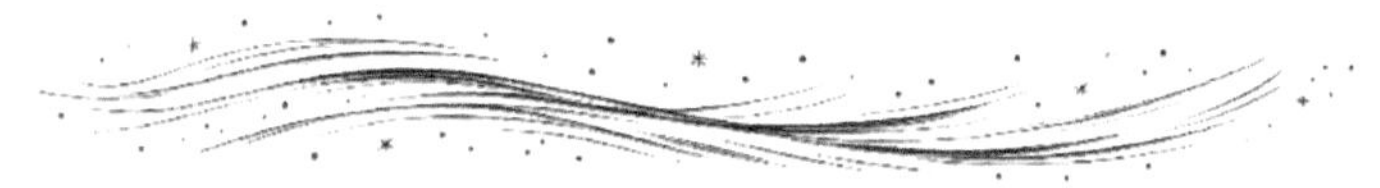

KIRA

I lay still for some time. The fur beneath me is soft and warm in the way only skin and the heat of a fireplace can make it. Above me, the ceiling shifts with shadows dancing across it from the flames flickering in the hearth.

Tom's breath warms the curve of my shoulder, slow and steady, like he is made for nights like these with me. One of his arms curls around my waist, the other is tucked under my neck, cradling me gently in a way I have never felt before.

Yet I don't feel as though I am caged here. Instead, my body aches in a good way: sore, heavy, and flushed from being taken wholly apart and put back together again. But deeper than that, beneath the heat that still thrums low in my belly, there is something else. Something quiet and whole. Like something quietly fractured in me and was loudly mended, with the touch and devotion of my mate.

I exhale, but the breath catches slightly in my throat because I didn't expect him. I didn't expect to be ensnared by a man in this lifetime.

When I kissed him, when I told him I didn't want to wait, I meant it. I wanted the choice, and he has let me have it since our first meeting. The clarity of saying yes and meaning it is the most powerful gift he could have ever given me. Even so, I didn't think it would feel like this. It feels like a weightless warmth and a sense of finally being seen.

When Tom touches me, it isn't like I am something to fix or claim. He hasn't rushed, hasn't forced, hasn't even leaned into the mate bond to let it take control like too many others would have.

And Goddess, when he moved inside me…

I curl into his chest tighter, taking in a larger breath than necessary, just enjoying his scent, his heat, him. His skin is warm beneath mine, and the curve of his chest is strong and solid against my cheek. The bond has been here constantly, and I can feel it in every heartbeat. Intense and terrifying all at once, but it hasn't swallowed me whole like I feared it would if I chanced to meet my mate. It hasn't taken my will or my choice. It simply exists now. Like another thing in the background, something very difficult to ignore, but still something we are choosing together.

'Still awake?' Tom murmurs against my hair, his voice low and rough.

I nod into his chest. The furs shift as he adjusts slightly, tucking the warmth of it higher over us. 'You're quiet.' 'I'm thinking,' I reply.

'About?' he asks, a soft curiosity in his tone.

I pause. I feel the instinct, sharp as ever, no matter how old it is, to keep the response to myself. But it passes quicker than it ever has before, like a shadow in the furthest corner of my mind.

You can give a little here, Kira, Sylvie pops into my mind.

I absolutely adore hearing her voice within me again. I have missed her dearly and can't imagine life without her again, and I can't thank the Greyfall pack enough for bringing her back to me.

He has shown you nothing but devotion and understanding, she finishes.

'About how I thought this would feel more like losing control, like losing oneself in place of another,' I say. 'But it doesn't feel that way at all.'

His hand moves slowly over my back, lazy and gentle, as if my skin is something he didn't want to rush through either. He was grounding in his movements, calming even.

'You were never out of control,' he says quietly. 'Not once.'

That undoes me. Not tears, but just the overwhelming connection between us. I bury my face in his chest to hide the tears that are pricking at the corners of my eyes.

Tom stays silent, holding me steady while the heat in my face and chest softens again, the emotions fading slowly.

'I didn't think I'd want this. Didn't think I deserved it.' I whisper, finally feeling controlled enough to speak. 'I didn't think I would want you. Not like this. I had every intention of rejecting you when the snap happened. Only I didn't know your name.' I confess.

'I know,' he says confidently. The way he said it was not possessive, not angry, just honest.

I tilt my head up to look at him; the firelight accentuating a scar along his jaw. I press my hand to his chest, right over the steady thumping of his heart. It was fast, but not frantic. Strong, but not overwhelming. It feels comfortable, like him.

'You're different,' I say, not meaning to actually say it out loud. 'From every other male I've met, I mean.'

'I'd certainly hope so,' he murmurs, a slight possessiveness now creeping into his voice while a small grin ghosts his lips.

'No,' I said with a small, uncertain laugh. 'I mean it. They all made me feel like I have to give something up. My body. My pride. My silence. But you-'

Tom shakes his head gently. 'You never have to give me anything. Kira, you owe me nothing.'

The ache in my throat sharpens.

'Then why have you done everything for someone you don't even know?' I ask. I don't mean to say that out loud either, but it slips, and I may as well be honest with him. I am still waiting for the other shoe to drop.

Tom doesn't blink. 'Because I want to. You're mine.' His eyes flash with his wolf, and I see for the first time true possessiveness in his features. It shakes me more than anything else that has transpired between us. Because I believe him. He wants me.

I tuck my head back under his chin, curling fully into him, and his hand instantly comes back to me, resuming its slow, grounding motion like it is second nature to him.

We don't talk for a while. Tom kisses the top of my head now and then, lost in his own thoughts.

'How is it having Sylvie back?' he asks gently. 'I saw the shift in your eyes, the cloud over earlier when she contacted you. It must be a relief; I know I couldn't be without Lex.'

Something unlocks deep in my chest as I exhale; he wants to know about my wolf.

'It's amazing; I have missed her dearly, and I have you to thank for bringing us back together.' I say, looking up at him. 'I can't wait to be strong enough for us to run again.' I can't help but smile at the memory of running with Sylvie. She was so perfect, so fast and masterful in the forest.

'Well, my dear, you simply say the word and as soon as you are both strong enough, Lex and I will take you running.' Tom smiles down at me. 'I can't wait to see her.'

Chapter Seven

TOM

THE MOMENT WE CROSS the border into the Atticus Star Pack territory, I feel it.

Wrong.

Just wrong.

It isn't a loud or obvious thing, nothing a normal visiting envoy might call out in front of an Alpha's court. But it is here. A stillness that the trees don't belong, a quietness that invokes that neither do those living here of any kind. And beneath it all, a thick metallic scent of blood masked in pine and perfume.

I've lived long enough and fought in enough shadows and battles to know the stench of rot when I breathe it.

At the gate, the sentries bow low, formal and respectful. But their gazes never lift past our boots; their wolves are very quiet within them; it feels almost submissive by force, not by nature.

Helios clocks it too. I can see it in the way he squares his shoulders and the flicker of his jaw muscle where the tension is sitting.

The King of Greyfall is many things, but blind certainly isn't one of them. He doesn't say a word as we pass through the towering iron gates; he doesn't need to.

The cold stone halls echo as we walk. I take in the high-arched ceilings, which hold perfect symmetry. The walls are lined with gilded tapestries bearing the Star sigil; black and red with the mouth of a howling wolf in the middle of a ten-pointed star. I assume it is meant to inspire awe, or fear, and maybe command some form of respect. But all I feel are threats. Like the tapestries themselves have teeth, ready to open our throats.

Omega attendants wait near the entrance, each one dressed in very simple, soft pastel linen. Their eyes cast downwards and not daring to look up once as they offer us trays of what smells to be honeyed wine.

I watch their hands shake as I refuse the drink without a word.

Helios, on the other hand, takes a goblet and passes it to a nearby guard with a quiet nod, letting them all know we won't touch anything offered without it first being thoroughly tested by their own first.

Beside me, Kira is walking in silence, not hidden, but not fully ready to expose herself to her old pack. Her posture is loose but brittle, as though if anyone were to touch her, she might snap and take with her the skin of the offender. She hasn't said much since we left Greyfall. But her energy speaks volumes: tight, focused, and unforgiving.

I stay close, not shielding her, not drawing attention, but near enough that if she feels the need to anchor herself, I'm there.

Not everyone here looks at us as guests.

People track our movements, subtle but deliberate. All warriors reporting to their Alpha. They haven't met Helios yet.

They haven't decided how far they can push him. Until we see what they are willing to do in front of him, an unknown Alpha, we need to keep our wits about us because until they do, this place isn't safe; it's a test.

Kira tilts her head slightly. 'They clean the blood off the stones before guests arrive,' her voice is low, so only us close to her can hear.

My gaze drifts briefly to the courtyard, to the too-clean stone beneath our feet.

'Otherwise, it stays there as a warning to those who oppose the higher-ranking wolves.'

I can't answer; what is there to say to such monstrosities? But I am sure Kira can feel even just a fraction of my heart breaking within our bond.

Helios catches her words. I see the recognition flash in his eyes. The slow, contained burn of a man making calculations that have nothing to do with our performance of politics and everything to do with the desire for justice for those being so horribly wronged within the North.

The main corridor leads us toward the council chamber; it's lined with guards every ten feet who stand incredibly still like art pieces. Their expressions are blank, either very well trained or dead inside. Either way, they seem to be too cold to be real. A pack this quiet is either perfectly balanced and in sync across the board, something Helios and I have not yet been able to achieve within the Greyfall Pack... or it is exceptionally broken.

We turn a corner and I catch the faintest scent; blood, old and scrubbed with cleaning agents that are mixing into the depleted scent. I clench my jaw so tightly that it aches almost instantly.

Helios leans into me, 'You smell that too?' he asks, his voice low and controlled. I nod once. 'There are no children here,' he adds. 'Not one. We've passed dozens of wolves inside and outside, and there is no laughter, no small feet or happy children.'

'They don't let them roam,' Kira says softly, having listened in. 'Not until they are old enough to understand punishment, fear, and their place.'

My stomach turns. This isn't just a performance visit anymore. Helios' aura is brewing slightly higher, along with my own. The more we learn about this place, the more we know something up here needs to change. Desperately. For the future of everyone who lives here.

We finally arrive at the correct chamber doors, bloody tall, polished and inlaid with what looks to be silver runes. A show of wealth, or power, or possibly both. But only a show.

Helios raises his brow at me, and I give him a small nod.

The large door swings open slowly, and we step inside the room.

Let the reckoning begin.

Chapter Eight

TOM

THE DIGNITARY TALKS, THE dinner and accommodations are calm and somewhat expectantly obtuse. Everything has moved along as we imagined for our visit. Smooth and predictable, a standard host pack behaving exactly as they should: steady, composed, offering nothing beyond what is necessary to maintain the illusion of normalcy. For now.

The sky overhead is painted with the cold grey of impending snowfall, with light leaking weakly through the heavy clouds. The procession we are observing, like everything else here, is a spectacle. It is not unusual; packs often put on a display for visiting allies, but Atticus Star does nothing by halves. The Atticus Star banners ripple in the wind, red on black, the howling sigil raised high above the gathered assembly.

Many high ranked wolves stand like statues, contrasting terribly with omegas who stand like shadows, trying to melt into the surrounding walls.

I stand with Helios at the front, flanked by Kira on the other side, standing just a little behind me, ever so slightly shielded from the display before us. From a distance, it might look like unity with this pack, three wolves of high rank representing some form of peace and respect for these traditions. But we all know better.

I watch as the omega boys march forward, carrying their ceremonial flags. Their limbs are stiff with the effort, their expressions kept carefully blank. Eyes down and feet perfectly spaced.

One of them slips before our eyes, just a missed step. But his flag slips from his grasp and flutters to the ground as gasps fill the courtyard from every side except the Alpha's.

Everything and everyone freezes. Except for the boy who is scrambling, pale and panicked. His fingers fumble with the fallen flag as his eyes flick upward. Not to us.

To him. Alpha Aston doesn't move; he doesn't need to. The entire courtyard is still, like it is holding a collective breath. The weight of his gaze alone on this boy is enough to still the air, to press down on the courtyard until even breathing feels like a risk. The boy's whole body shakes harder under it. A muscle ticks in Aston's jaw. A single step forward echoes in the courtyard; the sound of it echoes far louder than it should, and the boy flinches like he's already been struck.

The Beta steps forward, face twisted in disgust. His cloak snaps behind him as he crosses the courtyard, not hurried, not uncertain. Deliberate and certainly not hidden. A ripple moves through the gathered wolves. This isn't a lapse in control; this is a choice.

Without warning or hesitation, his hand cracks sharply against the side of the boy's face. The sound is sharp and cruel as the boy crumples instantly, one hand flying to his cheek. No one moves or speaks; I don't think they would dare to after such an open display of cruelty.

But once the strike lands, and every eye shifts, every widened eye of the crowd, and every calculating one of the ranked members, even the Beta flashes up.

Not to the boy. Not to Alpha Aston. To Helios.

Still, no one moves. Helios hasn't reacted. I see it in him: the twitch of restraint in his jaw; the tension pressuring his already taut muscles, and the slight widening of his eyes in disbelief. We came here for proof of this pack's cruelty. Here it is, right in front of our extremely open eyes. Still, Lex growls beneath my skin, furious and protective. Every instinct I have is screaming at me to match their violence with violence.

Besides me, Kira doesn't flinch. Not visibly. But her hand curls into her cloak so tightly I can see her knuckles turning white against the dark material.

'This is what they do,' she whispers, her voice very raw with emotion.

The boy tries to rise again, but two guards appear at his side. One takes hold of his arms while the other takes hold of his collar. They don't guide him toward any of the buildings, not to any infirmary; instead, they turn toward a side path. Gravel and stone scraping his legs as he is dragged along it.

I turn slightly, just enough to study Kira's face. Her lips are pressed thin, her jaw is trembling slightly from how tightly she is holding it.

'Do you want to leave?' I ask her quietly.

She doesn't answer me, just turns on her heel and follows the young boy and the guards. No one stops us; the procession has ended abruptly with members like the alpha immediately leaving the area, and with all the movement, no one notices us heading in the same direction as them.

We follow them silently, the path curving behind the training barracks, away from the courtyard's public view. As we round the corner, the wind picks up, carrying with it the smell of sweat and blood.

The punishment yard looks to be carved into the bones of the earth. No paint. No flowers, or grass, or living things. Just cold, pitted stone that is stained darker in places where blood has dried too fast to be scrubbed completely clean.

I know this place from the memories Kira shared with me. I know it before I even see it. But it is much worse in person. The walls are so high, possibly too high for sound to even escape. The silence is by design.

The boy is already bound when we enter the grounds. His shirt has been torn away, his skin prickling from the cold air surrounding us. Leather cuffs have him connected to the pole through the rusted cast iron rings; the post itself was so worn and full of grooves from the many punishments that have been dealt before this one.

The wolf holding the whip is tall with clean robes. He doesn't announce the sentence, just lets the first lash split the air like thunder against the boy's skin with well-practised hands. The first and second lashes don't bring so much as a whimper from the boy whose eyes are blankly staring ahead of him. Under the third, his knees buckle beneath him, but somehow he holds himself up, still silent, like it is his will against the whip.

But the fourth strike lands with such brutal force that a scream rips from him.

Lex lunges in my chest, feral and sudden, snarling with a force that could have cracked my ribs from the inside. I stagger under the weight of it, clenching my fists, my claws pushing through my skin at the pain. Helios shifts beside me, ready to intervene, but waits. This is why we are here.

To see.

To be seen.

Kira moves. I don't have to say anything but just follow in protective instinct half a step behind her, an instinct as natural as breathing.

The whip rises before us, and Kira moves before I can stop her. Not fast enough to be reckless, but definitely not slow enough for her to be cautious.

'Is this your idea of justice?' Her voice cuts through the still air, echoing around the area.

The whip freezes mid-air; the strike suspended by her daring.

All eyes turn to Kira. The guards, the council witnesses. The other wolves being forced to watch the punishment as some sick way of reminding them to behave and do as ordered, exactly as ordered.

Kira steps forward and reaches up to her hood, pulling it down.

'I have been tied to that post on three occasions,' her voice carries to them all. 'Once, for disobeying the Alpha's order to kneel. Once for shielding another from a far worse punishment. And once, because I had tried to run, tried to escape. I survived all three. But other wolves didn't, and you will all answer for every one of those deaths.' Kira's eyes are fierce and focused on the council witnesses in particular. The higher ranks that allow such cruelty.

I move beside Kira, close enough that our shoulders just brush each other. Not in front of her, not behind her, but with her.

The wolf with the whip takes a step back as Helios steps forward.

No crown on his head, no banner behind him. Just his presence, authority so ingrained it makes lesser wolves instinctively bow their heads.

'The King of Greyfall bears witness to this punishment,' he states.

His voice isn't raised, nor is he threatening. His announcement isn't passive; for Helios, it's a declaration. And it means, if they are to continue now… if they lay one more lashing on that boy's back… Helios will not hold back on the one who holds the whip, or passes the punishment.

'The pain,' Helios' voice now low and final. 'Will be answered by your council in kind.' The weight of his sentence hangs in the air, suspended in the face of people who had not expected an outsider to step in.

The first to move is a young omega attendant who sprints to the post. Her hands unshackle the cuffs from the boy's wrists, letting him sag into her arms, bleeding and silent. He still doesn't cry. He just watches Kira with wide eyes.

Kira turns away first, walking out of the yard with her head held high. I follow her into the shadows beyond the courtyard. The torchlights here flickering around us.

'Are you okay?' I ask and she stops walking.

She doesn't answer, just exhales. One breath, and then two. Her hands are clenched tightly at her sides. But when I reach for one, she allows me to take it. I run my fingers along hers, feeling the tension deep in her skin.

'You didn't stop it,' she says quietly, not looking at me.

'I couldn't,' I reply. 'Not until Helios got what he needed. He needed them to show us who they are.'

Kira nods once, and for the first time since we entered the Atticus Star territory, she leans into me. Her full weight pressing against me with a need to be grounded in the moment.

I wrap my arm around her shoulders and press my forehead to hers, and I hold her close and tight.

Tighter than I have ever held anything. Because if I let her go, I might lose her.

I am not sure I would survive that; I can't lose her now that I have her.

Chapter Nine

TOM

HELIOS CATCHES UP TO us, but we barely move five steps when Alpha Aston appears in front of us, not approaching us, no greeting, but rather blocking our exit.

Tall, broad, wearing a smile that people wear when they are too used to getting their way and being unchallenged. The alpha steps into our path like he owns everything about the scene: the ground, the sky… us. Stepping as close as he could to show his intent in his challenge.

'That was a mistake, Boy-King.' His voice is sharp, his anger bleeding into it.

Helios stands tall beside me. Not a flinch, not a blink, just absolute stillness, which causes the alpha to take a second measure of him.

I know Helios; I know the stillness that he surrounds himself with. It's like his own type of armour. The last time I saw it on him was mere moments before he had to kill his own father.

'Was it?' Helios asks evenly, his voice smooth but his aura pulsing around us.

Alpha Aston rolls his shoulder and takes yet another step closer to Helios, his coat shifting on his shoulders, his aura darkening in a very unsubtle and very disrespectful manner.

'I don't recognise your rule here,' he says, his voice raising quickly. 'You have no sovereignty in the North. You walk here as a guest, and you interfere in matters which are not yours.'

The air thickens around us with the growing of the two auras. It isn't magic; this is wolves. Pure, dominant pressure radiating from two wolves who are not used to hearing the word 'no'.

Power bleeds from Helios in very slow, precise waves. His control and discipline are a staunch reminder of his position above other wolves. But Alpha Aston, his power is from a younger bloodline. Wilder. His aura is lashing out like claws on glass. Sharp and untested.

I feel Lex rise under my skin, our hairs prickling in the charged air. His teeth want to bare, claws to lengthen, that is our best friend, but more importantly, that is our king being challenged.

Kira stands behind me; I can feel her tension also, the two auras affecting her physically, yet she stands silently with us.

Helios takes a step forward, and the ground seems to tremble.

'You forget yourself,' he says, still calm. 'I bear a title given by blood and rite. The seat of Greyfall is not just a southern throne; it is the centre of the were species sovereignty.'

Alpha Aston sneers, 'By whose word? Yours?'

'By the blood of the First Fang, born of the Moon Goddess,'

Helios says. 'By the oaths of your ancestors who swore when the moon split the sky and carved the territories. By the Moon Goddess herself.' As Helios talks, his aura grows and slowly the alpha's shoulders begin to round, his head slightly getting lower.

And just like that, Helios drops the hammer of history between them.

For a heartbeat, I think the Alpha might bow. Might recall the law burned into our bones. Instead, he fights the king's aura and bared his throat, not in submission but in a challenge. And I watch the slow grin split across Helios' face.

He steps forward again, bending slightly to be nose to nose with Aston, letting his Lycan shift bleed through just enough to darken the whites of his eyes and lengthen his canines.

'You want a challenge?' Helios says softly. 'Be careful, I haven't had a reason to stretch my claws recently.'

Alpha Aston growls low, and for a moment, I think we are about to have a war here before dinner. But then the Beta, a lean and older wolf with scars running from his temple to under his shirt collar, steps up from behind the alpha and places a firm hand on his shoulder.

'Not now,' he says in warning. 'Not in front of the court.' For a long moment, Aston doesn't move.

Then, finally, he steps back. Not a full retreat, but enough to show he is conceding, for now.

He turns his gaze steadily to Kira, a flicker of recognition in his eyes and a snarl on his lips. Not an ounce of surprise either; he knew she had been here the whole time. He just didn't acknowledge it until now.

'And what is this?' he says softly. Before anyone can react, he steps sideways, straight past Helios. Straight to Kira, too close for my liking.

'You bring my own strays back into my court?' he murmurs.

Lex surges violently beneath my skin. But Helios moves first, fastest. In a single step, he places himself back between them both, a wall of protection in front of Kira, and the air intensifies as Alpha Aston's aura flickers with his anger that lashes out directly at Helios.

'Careful,' Helios says quietly.

'You were almost something valuable here,' Aston says softly, focusing back on Kira. 'Such a waste. You've made your point,' Alpha Aston says tightly. 'Now get the fuck out of my territory. If I catch any of you here again,' his eyes bore into Kira over Helios' shoulder. 'I will have you put down.'

Stalking off with his beta, they vanish into the shadows along the path.

Helios rolls his shoulders once, calm and controlled. But I can see the rage boiling under his skin. The tension shifting between him and Lucifer is clear in their eyes.

He doesn't look at me, just says, 'We're done here.'

For the first time since we arrived, I know, without a doubt, that Atticus Star is going to burn.

Chapter Ten

TOM

THE SNOW IS FALLING again as we pass the last ridge, fine and silver, the kind that will melt before it can land on the ground. It catches in Kira's hair here and there and clings to the shoulders of my cloak, softening the world until even the trees feel quiet in the slight breeze. Every step of the horses' hooves is muffled in the growing hush surrounding us.

She rides next to me. Close enough that I can hear the rhythm of her breathing, not shallow, not panicked, just measured and controlled. Like everything about her lately. We haven't spoken since we left Atticus Star. There hasn't been a need. The silence between us isn't uncomfortable; it is heavy, yes, but full of the same unspoken bond that has now carried us both through the confrontation together. After what we witnessed, words seem so small.

But Goddess, the silence gives my mind too much room to roam.

I keep seeing the boy's face. The whip and the stillness after. And of course, the Alpha, nose to nose with Helios, just daring him. Lex hasn't stopped pacing in my mind since. His gruffness and tension runs through me.

When Greyfall rises from the mist, I exhale fully. Not relief, but something close to. We are home and Kira is still next to me.

Home.

The gates open for us without question, the guards barely offering salutes. They can see it on our faces, smell it on our clothes. War isn't coming; it has already begun.

Kira slides from her saddle with no need of help. She still doesn't speak, but she walks close beside me as we pass through the stone corridors. Every servant and soldier we pass step aside, not out of deference, but out of respect. The war chamber is already lit when we arrive, Helios had already sent word ahead of us. The fire is roaring; the lanterns are spilling golden light over the maps, scrolls and intelligence already being supplied. Helios steps up to the centre, both hands bracing against the carved edges of the table.

Helios looks up as we take our places, and I see the shift within him. The weight that drops behind his eyes. Not fear or doubt, but determination and ferocity.

'It's worse than we thought,' I say. 'It's not simply tradition that they are living. It's tyranny. Calculated and structured to keep their people in place.' Helios nods slowly.

Kira steps forward, her voice quiet, but despite that, it carries around the room. 'A child. Thirteen, maybe, in a public beating with no resistance. This is a normal routine for the people of the Atticus Star Pack. Its routine cruelty.'

Helios' jaw flexes. 'And the Alpha?' he presses.

'He challenged you,' she says, her voice low. 'Said himself he doesn't recognise you as a king within his borders.'

'Yes. I think we need to remind him,' Helios states simply.

Silence falls within the room again. I step up beside the table, brushing my fingers across the edge of a map that displays the northern border where the Atticus Star territory begins. Their crimson sigil marking the paper in dark ink, and I lay my hand flat over the top of the insulting symbol.

'This is bigger than just Kira,' I say. 'More than some petty revenge. That pack is a symptom of rot within the kingdom, and it will spread through the bloodlines. If we let this go, let it fester, if we let that boy's blood dry without an uproar, we are telling every alpha they are untouchable, even by the king. That they can treat their packs however they want. Just like they did under your father's rule.'

Helios looks at me intently, his eyes flashing with Lucifer's golden hue.

'Are you ready to go back into a battle?' Helios asks.

He's referring to the one we undertook to secure him the crown, and honestly, I would do that and this battle every day until my last breath if it meant destroying the bad lines in our territories.

'I'm ready for another war.' I reply.

Helios nods sharply, 'Right, then we move now, before the snow seals the pass to the north.'

Kira draws closer to the table. Her fingers hovering above the marked villages near the Atticus border.

'Their strength is in fear, as you've seen,' she says flatly. 'But that fear has to be maintained and held together by consistent and ongoing punishment and displays of cruelty. If you break the fear, you break their control.'

I watch her with pride. She isn't just surviving here; she is planning, strategizing, and finding her place.

Helios can see it too, as he inclines his head toward her. 'Then we strike where it counts. But we will need the people with us, not just as witnesses but as allies. You're going to have to lead that outreach.'

Kira nods her head firmly; mission accepted.

I step toward Kira as the room fills with movement and rustling.

'Do you believe we will win this?' she asks hesitantly and quietly to not let Helios hear her.

I nod.

'We're not just going to win,' I say. 'We are going to destroy them for what they have put you and all the others through.'

Her lips form a faint curve. 'Good.'

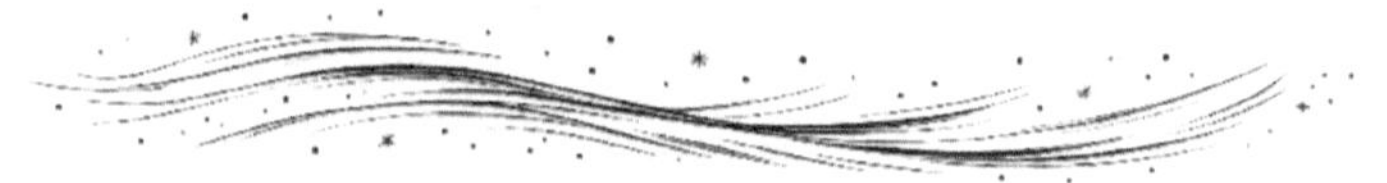

KIRA

The fire continues low in the hearth, its glow casting sharp shadows up the stone walls of the chamber. I pace the floor, arms crossed and boots almost silent against the worn stone. It seems this room has been used quite a lot, and that is worrisome for a 'war chamber'.

Tom stands to my left, silent but present; his energy is much more stable than mine, grounded and watchful rather than feeling the need to move. Helios stands at the head of the map table, head bowed, fingertips pressing into the parchments like he is already bracing for the impact of the impending battle.

Many others have since joined us: scribes, messengers, and those who I assume are here to advise the king on these types of discussions and decisions.

'Kira, what are the Atticus forces like? What do you know of their barracks?' Helios asks, lifting his head to look me in the eye while speaking to me.

'What you saw before?' I shake my head slightly. 'That wasn't strength. That was just theatre. This is different. They have numbers, and they hold formation well, only it isn't mutual unity. It's fear keeping them in line.'

Tom's head flicks up to me.

'Aston doesn't need loyalty. He just needs them to believe that failing him is worse than dying for him.' I inform them. 'And wolves like that don't break cleanly… they lash out.'

I exhale slowly. It really is no way for any wolf to be living its life. 'So, this isn't about territory,' I continue. 'It's about his control.' My jaw tightens as I glance toward Tom. 'He had a place for me, and I tore it apart just by surviving him, showing it can be done.' I say as I exhale slowly.

'If he walks away now… he doesn't just lose power; he will prove he never had it.' Helios chimes in.

I move close to Helios and the map, fingers hovering over the northern quadrant where familiar roads, posts, and stations are marked in neat, inked lines. My body knows every path; my senses still remember the feel of them, the scents.

'These here,' I point to three circular marks along the outer ring within the stronghold, 'are military posts. These are always manned. Always. The alpha has made sure visitors see a full rotation. Guards in formation, clean uniforms and dutiful soldiers, as you would remember. They have the strength and the need to survive and win.'

A flicker of fire catches in Helios' eyes. He doesn't interrupt me, just watches intently.

'Alpha Aston sends his warriors to control omegas around his territory and makes sure to guard borders and the stronghold. I don't think he would ever believe someone would dare to challenge him, though.'

Tom shifts, and I sense the storm of emotions passing through our bond. The feeling is something so unnatural yet natural all at the same time. I can only imagine what it will be like when we are able to fully relish in a full bond connection after we mark each other in time.

'You saw the fear in their faces,' I say, looking between the two of them. 'The way the guards wouldn't meet our eyes. How the omegas flinch at a closing door. It's the worse type of conditioning. It won't take much, just a spark of defiance. One sign that the alpha is not invincible, that he will be held accountable.'

Finally, Tom speaks up. 'You really believe if we go in, the omegas are going to rise against their torturers?'

'Maybe not all of them, but some. Enough to disrupt his hold over them all and hopefully tip the balance in our favour.' I can feel the snarl rising.

He is not meaning to question you and the ability of the omegas, Sylvie's voice calmly reminds me. *He's wanting to ensure that when they go in, they can protect themselves, but also those vulnerable in there.* I know she is right and relax my fists that have curled in frustration.

Helios exhales loudly through his nose as he steps away from the table, closer to the fire where the flames highlight just how young he is.

'If I declare war,' he says carefully to everyone in the room. 'I won't just be retaliating. I'll be claiming complete dominance over the territory. I will take the entire north by this show of force.'

'You'll be challenging the alpha himself, openly. You will have no choice but to take it after that.' Tom's voice is dark with something I haven't heard in him before, and a weight seems to fill the chamber.

I meet Helios' gaze and keep it, stepping close to the fire alongside him. 'You need to do it.'

'You both realise, this won't end with just a border skirmish or a battle in the stronghold?' Helios looks between me and Tom.

'We know,' Tom says, and I nod in agreement.

Helios stares into the fire for a long moment.

'If I let this stand,' he continues, quieter now. 'If I allow a pack to defy the throne openly, to take what they want and call it law…' His jaw tightens. 'Then I don't have a realm.' He turns from the fire, stepping back to the table. His hand hovers over the map for just a fraction of a second, then he picks up a small, weighted stone from the map and moves it. North. Directly into the heart of the Atticus Star territory.

'We leave in five days,' he says with finality.

I meet his gaze without hesitation. 'Absolutely.'

Tom steps closer, filling the space between Helios and me, his eyes piercing mine. 'You understand this could make you a target for the alpha,' he states softly.

'I became a target to that man a long time ago, the first time I said no to him,' I answer.

Tom reaches out, fingers brushing against the skin of my hand softly.

Helios turns away, already issuing instructions to those present. Whilst Tom stays closer to me, his voice low enough that no one else can hear him.

'Lucky you survived that place long enough to burn it to the ground yourself.' He's right.

This time, when I walk into that cursed pack, I won't be alone. It will be with fire at my back and the full weight of Greyfall ready to strike.

I just hope I get to see the light leave the alpha's eyes.

The corridor is cold beneath my bare feet, the chill grounding me. Greyfall is hushed tonight, the kind that comes after movement and decision making.

I stand with my hands braced on the cool windowsill, forehead resting against the glass. I'm not sure how long I have been here. Long enough for the firelight in the hall to dim in the brackets. Long enough for the weight of the decisions made today to sink deeply into my bones.

I hear Tom before I see him, not because he's loud, but because everything else seems to quiet when he moves. He stops just behind me, the insides of his feet gently pressing against the outsides of mine, his voice raspy in the darkening corridor.

'You okay?'

I close my eyes and really try to think about the answer to such a loaded question. Tom's breath is slow and quiet, the warmth brushing against my neck, eliciting a desire to feel his lips on my skin. The bond tugs faintly between us, humming beneath my skin, a warmth flaring within me.

'What if I am not ready to go back there and see it burn?' I ask without opening my eyes.

Earlier, my voice had been so clear; I was so confident. Burn it all down, make them feel even a fraction of what they did to me. Make Alpha Aston realise what fear truly is. But here, in the quiet, in the safety and warmth of the packhouse, here with Tom, I hesitate. Because I know exactly what it is going to take to destroy a place like Atticus Star, and I don't know if I can do it without becoming just like them.

'You don't have to be ready, Kira,' Tom says gently, his lips right under my earlobe. 'You just have to walk with me.' Slowly, I turn to face him, leaning on the windowsill.

He looks tired. Not worn down, but stretched a little thin at the moment. His steel-grey eyes have a raw calmness beneath them, but they also show a darkness within, accompanied by a sleep deprived set of circles around them. When our eyes meet, the pull is there again. The gravity tugging us together from the moment we collided in the snow.

Except this time, it isn't just the heat of the bond. It's also a desire from me to him and vice versa. A want to be touched and held by him. Caressed, loved, and completely devoured by this incredible wolf that I have been sent from the Moon Goddess herself.

Tom lifts his hand and tucks a stray hair behind my ear, his fingers brushing my jaw carefully. I can't help but lean into his touch before I can stop myself. His thumb traces the curve of my cheek. He doesn't smile or speak, just leans forward until his forehead is touching mine.

The breath catches in my throat. A heady need growing with his presence. I can feel the fear within me still, but with Tom's steady breath against mine, and the weight of an unspoken promise, the fear isn't drowning me in my mind. The noise in my head fades; the constant what-ifs finally quiet. I nod against him; his determination boosts mine, and once again, I can do this. I need to do this for those still left in the hands of those demented people of Atticus Star.

Tom exhales slowly with me.

'We do this together,' his confirmation building my confidence within us as a mated pair.

I nod once again, unable to string two words together.

If I am going to walk back into the place that broke me, I will not do it as the girl who escaped.

I leave the corridor long before the sun even thinks about rising. Retreating to the warm safety of our room for an uneasy rest. Because before the first light touches Greyfall, I will make my way to the training yard.

Chapter Eleven

TOM

I FIND HER IN the training yard before dawn.

The courtyard is silver-washed in moonlight; the snow on the ground around the sparring ring is trampled down by those who rise early to begin preparations for the day here. But there is no one else in sight, just her.

Kira stands at the centre of the ring, feet bare and braced against the cold, her muscles taut beneath her fitted top and her breath coming in short pants, visible in the cool air. Her braid hangs down her back, and in her hand is a simple blade. I know her and Sylvie have been able to talk and have reconnected, but there is something holding them back from an actual shift. So, for now it seems, Kira is making sure she can manoeuvre herself with a weapon, since her most valuable one is not strong enough yet.

She moves through motions slowly at first, each step methodical and balanced. She has excellent footwork, but I can feel the tension growing in her: frustration and what I think is fear.

Kira lunges and twists before pivoting straight back into her stance. She doesn't waste any energy with her movements, even though she was captive for so long. She was at one point taught to fight, and against herself and the empty ring, she doesn't hesitate.

I wait in the shadows, not wanting to interrupt her training. Her breath is the only sound in the early morning as she darts around in a display of graceful movement not meant for prying eyes like mine. Until she finishes a sequence and turns directly to me, her eyes blazing with determination.

'How long have you been here?' she asks directly.

'Long enough,' I reply, stepping forward from the wall. Her face falls. 'Since you're second form, I think,' I give her a warm smile. 'That lunge was clean. But you dip your right elbow too far before the turn, someone could-' I reach out without warning and grab hold of her elbow, spinning her around so her back is pressed to my chest with her arm twisted up between us.

Kira lets out a short huff when we collide.

'You're going to correct me?' she asks, twisting her wrist that is firmly in my grasp.

'You're not one for false comfort,' I purr into her ear, I can feel the change in her demeanour, the touch, my proximity; she needs it all as much as I do, with our bond not yet sealed.

'No, I really don't,' she replies gently, before swinging her arm in my grasp down and breaking the hold I had on her. My boots crunch the snow as I follow her into the ring.

'Who taught you to fight?' I ask. She has definitely had someone experienced in her life.

'My father,' she says so low I nearly miss it, it's clearly a comment she is not wishing to have dissected here this morning.

'Well, shall we see what you do with an opponent in front of you?' I smile across at her widened eyes.

I enjoy her not seeing this coming.

She barely nods before launching at me. The sparring match itself is intense, almost like a calibration of movement for me, where I can see how she fights, what weaknesses she looks out for to capitalise on, and what weaknesses she is trying desperately to hide from me.

We find a steady rhythm fast as she also adjusts her stance on instinct, watching for my tells and attempting to read my movements before I make them. Which foot has more weight in it, the back or the front?

Goddess, she is quick and strong. I can see why the Moon Goddess fated me to such a firecracker. This is the type of woman I will gladly go to war for, over and over again.

She strikes sharply with a stable core and quick recovery that would put some of our warriors to shame. She pivots cleanly, never overreaching, with every strike snapping back before I can counter. Every pass between us is made with discipline, and every time she connects with me, the sting is immediate, and her smile grows each time. Infectious and beautiful on such a frigid morning, it throws me off more than the strike itself.

I finally lock her wrists mid-strike, both panting, her cheeks flushed and my heartbeat punching so hard beneath my ribs, it's almost painful. Her eyes glare up into mine as she immediately tugs at her wrists, but I have her firmly in my hands right now, and I have absolutely no intention of letting her back away from me now. She twists to pull free, and I tighten my grip without thinking, holding her to me, closer than either of us was a second ago.

'You're quite terrifying, you know?' I tell her, unable to keep the amusement out of my voice.

I'm not laughing at her, though; I am enthralled by her. Her skill, her speed, and her absolutely on point strikes, which will eliminate any slower wolves in her path.

She smirks up at me. 'Good, I want to be terrifying.'

Releasing her, I wrap an arm around her shoulders and draw her close to my side. Walking over to her boots and sitting under the continuously growing oak at the edge of the courtyard, still breathing heavily but at peace in each other's company.

Sweat clings to the back of my neck, cooling slowly in the air. Kira's hair is damp and sticks to her temple; her eyes trained out on something further into the distance beyond the courtyard. She looks radiant in the morning glow as the moon begins making way for the sun.

It's generally easy to keep a steady silence with Kira; I should be able to sit with her here, in our bubble of exhaustion, and let the air close around us and bring us easily together for warmth. But as I watch her putting her boots back on, it's no longer easy to remain silent.

'I was an orphan,' I say the words far quieter than I mean them to be.

She has told me her nightmare of a life; it's time I give her something in return. I don't look at her though. As soon as I say it, her head flicks toward me, not putting any pressure on, but just intently listening for what is going to follow such a conversation starter.

'I grew up thinking I was weak, or defective in some way… Definitely unwanted,' I continue looking at the ground. 'I was small and alone. I first shifted with Lex when I was only around eight years old. Everyone I knew back then thought I would have been dead before ever meeting my wolf.' I take a deep, steadying breath. 'When he came, Lex nearly tore me completely apart. For a very long time, we didn't have any kind of rhythm to our shifts, and it was incredibly painful every time. Eight-year-olds aren't made to shift,' I state.

I remember the pain like it lives beneath my skin. The wild panic of a first shift compressed with the agony of every single bone breaking all at once and not understanding why or what to do with the pain.

Kira glances sideways at me, her voice very quiet. 'But you survived it, that life. The early introduction to your wolf.'

'I would not be here today if Lex had not rescued me when he did,' I admit. 'He came to me early and painfully. But he made sure I was warm at night; made sure I could hunt and eat.'

Admiration leaks into my voice as I remember the first time I heard him. *Goddess, you're a scrawny little thing, but we will make do with you.*

'I don't think I was meant to survive, really.' I stare out at the tree line, letting the breeze that's picking up cool the heat in my chest. 'Even after I was made Beta by Helios, I just kept on thinking how someone was going to figure out that I am not enough. Waited for some time for Helios to realise he had made a mistake.'

'Sounds like Helios knew exactly what he was doing. You only have to listen to him when he speaks to you,' she says, so softly

I could have missed it. 'He loves you dearly.'

I look at her, really take her in. She doesn't look back at me right away.

Never in a million years would I have called what is between me and Helios love. Not like that.

She finishes pulling her boots on and leans into my shoulder, and I let my head gently rest on the top of hers. The air between us shifts; I can smell her. Salt, warmth and peonies, the sweetest scent I could ever have in my life ever again.

Chapter Twelve

TOM

HELIOS STANDS AT THE head of the table, shoulders squared. His fingers are steepled in front of him; his jaw is tensed in a sharp line. His gaze sweeps the room slowly, taking in every one of the faces in front of him, every piece of resistance and hesitation.

The elders are already seated, five in total. A council of traditions, memories of the packs and long bloodlines that have filled the seats, one after another from the same families. They all wear the same thing: ceremonial robes which look far too heavy for the state of their aging and fragile looking bodies. They sit in high-backed chairs, unlike the rest of us who they seem to think are below them; the large seats seeming like they are carved from the very stones that line the walls of the chamber.

I stand behind Helios' right shoulder, currently the only place for me to be in the room.

'Atticus Star,' Helios begins, his voice even. 'Their system of power is built on oppression. Cruelty even. We saw this firsthand when their alpha allowed an unarmed child to be disciplined in front of us. Their punishment yard still stains the stones red, and their omegas walked with their heads bowed to all who walk into the pack grounds, and their backs carry the scars of their transgressions.'

The room absorbs his words in silence, the particular silence that I have learned, in a very short period, means the elders are not currently in contemplation, but delaying.

The Elder Sconce, who is tall with a long white beard and is probably older than most of the trees in the forest that surrounds us, clears his throat. 'We don't deny that the abuse has occurred. But to commence an open conflict over another pack's internal customs-'

'Customs?' I snap before I can stop myself, my voice wracking the room. Every head turns toward me. 'You call public whippings, forced bondings and enslaved omegas customs?'

Sconce holds my eye, slowly blinking at me like I am a child throwing a tantrum over something insignificant. But Helios doesn't stop me, doesn't even take the moment to glance back at me. So, I keep going.

'They brutalise their own, train submission into their children. One of their own omegas came here, bleeding and half-dead; she is only one out of hundreds. We know it. We all fucking know it. You've seen the reports. What more do you need? Photographic proof? The body count? I am positive it would be massive!' A heavy, sharp-edged silence blankets the room.

Sconce's voice remains maddeningly calm. 'I'm not saying we don't act. I'm saying we proceed carefully. A declaration of war against Atticus Star will set a precedent. Greyfall has never sought dominion over the other territories to the north; we would become what you are claiming to oppose.'

'We wouldn't be conquering,' Helios says, his voice calm but threaded with something else, something darker and pointed at Sconce. 'We'd be liberating.'

'And absorbing,' another of the elders murmur. 'Their land, their wolves and their resources. The bloodlines carried through the ages. You would stretch our reach far into the north, where we could never hold. This changes everything about going into open war.'

There it is.

It isn't a fear of war that has the elders scrambling to create a delay in our movements, but a fear of what the war will require and the changes that will be inevitable. Change is something positively terrifying to those who have felt too comfortable for too long.

The scent of fear clings to these old men who are trying to cling to *their* balance, *their* way of life, and desperately clinging to *their* old king.

Helios' voice drops, 'If we turn a blind eye now, we will become complicit. You know that. You would all prefer me to be my father.'

The room chills instant at the insinuation.

'We propose diplomacy, my king,' Sconce replies slowly, picking his words carefully. 'A longer alliance, conditional aid, leverage. We should apply pressure from within. Undermine the alpha's support and eventually the system will fracture, and they will be forced to reform for their own survival.' I laugh; I can't help it.

'While omegas starve? While children are literally groomed for the chain? You want to take years for a possibility, not a guaranteed outcome, while so many suffer.'

Sconce doesn't answer; he honestly doesn't need to.

The answer will always be to delay with them; this council would rather bury their heads in the sand.

Helios leans forward, both palms laying out flat on the map strewed table. 'Atticus Star is a wound that will rot and fester and spread if we don't act immediately and cut it out.'

'And if you fail, young king?' Sconce asks accusatorily as though that was a guaranteed outcome. 'What then, King Helios? What if your forces fail? What if the northern packs unite against you? The north is as large as the south and had been practically ruled by Atticus Star for its entire existence. So if you do not succeed, will you continue to call it a liberation effort if your own borders of Greyfall burn as a result?'

The silence falls again, only this time it feels even colder, if that is possible. Helios turns to me; it's not a question, he's letting me know he has it, the answer.

'Well,' Helios begins in an exceptionally calm and measured voice. 'If you cannot support this choice,' his eyes turn to each elder. 'Then all of you are free to step down. I will not be the king who stands by letting another pack rot in silence. I will happily remove your titles and replace you tomorrow.'

The room shifts completely. It feels as though a physical manifestation of power shifting sides has hit us all. Helios does not wait for a yes or no from them all; he is, after all, a man of action, one this council has severely underestimated.

I watch Sconce look down at his hands for the first time, looking unsure of himself. I watch the other elders fold their arms, shift uncomfortably as if they've just realised their most important mistake: Helios is not his father, and maybe their time is up.

KIRA

I didn't mean to overhear. The corridors near the war chamber are drafty, chilled by the stone and silence they have endured for so long. I'd been walking them out of restlessness more than anything, finding it hard to remain in the rooms they have given to me. Too quiet in there, too soft. I need movement; I need something solid beneath my feet to keep me grounded; the stones are much more like the home I am used to.

But then I hear his voice.

Tom.

Low, frustrated, with more of an edge to it than I have ever heard. The kind of sound that isn't meant to bring comfort, but instead, break walls down. I slow, pressing my fingers to the carved edging of the archway, staying just out of sight, but well within hearing range.

Inside, the voices rumble, distant but clear.

'She is the catalyst,' someone was saying in a clipped tone, dismissive even. 'You wouldn't be talking about open war like this if not for the she-wolf; you wouldn't even know of the

Atticus Star issues.'

The words slice me like one of the many whippings I have endured. *Catalyst.*

Another voice, equally harsh, 'And now we'll send hundred to die for one she-wolf's trauma.' My stomach twists.

As if my survival has forced their hands. As if my very existence has upended their peace here in Greyfall. The quiet logic of it all settles in my chest like a poison: If I hadn't escaped, hadn't shown up here and spoken out, if I hadn't been found, there would be no war. I have disrupted everything for these men who have been living their luxurious lives of peace.

My legs tremble and I slide my hand from the archway, not feeling my fingers. Inside the room, the voices continue, lower now, murmured words, words I can't catch. But I don't need to know any more. The damage has already been done.

I back away carefully from the chamber, slow and careful to not cause any noise that might alert them all to my presence. The corridor seems even cooler now; my steps seem to be heavier and echoing louder the further away I get from those men.

I walk until I find a little alcove near the eastern terrace. The stone bench catches the last warmth of the sun as I sit still, arms locked tight around my legs; my grip doesn't loosen, something underneath it won't settle. My body feels strong and steady. But my insides are unravelling, churning with what I overheard.

They will never say it. Never admit it to me, not even Tom, whose voice I have grown to trust sometimes more than my own. He will say it is blanketed justice, that what is coming has always been inevitable. My jaw tightens while I stare at my boots.

But the worst part of it all is the small voice in the back of my mind, bitter and agreeable with those old men. A voice which is whispering to me, *if you hadn't run*, I squeeze my eyes shut, wishing the voice to be quiet. *If you hadn't said anything, none of this would be happening. If you hadn't spoken, none of these wolves would be going to war to die.*

I dig my nails into my palms until crescent moons bloom on my skin, but I cannot cry. Crying would be an acknowledgement. And agreement, a weakness.

Instead, I sit here on the stone bench until the sun dips low enough to burn gold along the tops of the trees in front of me. Until my body has stopped shaking and I can breathe once again without tasting the ash of the words that continue to replay in my mind.

Only then do I let my feet take me back, back to the room that is too quiet, too comfortable and entirely too much for a runaway rogue like me.

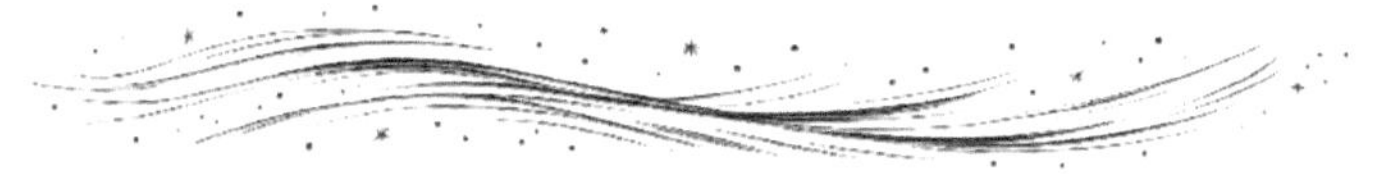

TOM

The heavy oak doors of the war chamber groan shut behind the last of the elders. The last echo of their footsteps fades into the silence, leaving behind a room steeped in the stillness that only comes after the last thread of any decency has completely dissolved. It is time for a fresh council; I daresay.

Helios is across from me, his palms still planted on the map table, knuckles pale from pressure. His jaw is tight and his eyes are fixed on the sprawling topography before him like he can will it to obey him. Smoke from the low burning fire curls into the roof, the scent of ash and old parchments pressing into my nose, mingling with the sour stench of disappointment.

Helios doesn't move for a long moment.

'They obviously will not back you,' I say, my voice certain.

He looks up at me. 'I never expected them to.'

There it is, no frustration from him, no anger. Just certainty.

I step forward, my boots echoing softly against the stone floor, each stride echoing around the empty chamber. 'Then this is it,' I say. 'You're really going to do this.' 'We are,' Helios replies bluntly.

'We need to do this properly,' I say, pacing slowly around the table, my eyes scanning the jagged line of the northern border, tracing every ridge and outpost position. 'The North won't fall easily. Atticus Star's defence will be difficult.' I pause, resting both hands on the edge of the table on the opposite side to Helios.

Helios' eyes narrow in thought. He leans back from the table, crossing his arms.

'H, I don't do this very often, but tonight, as your Beta, you need to go to bed. Go.' I say sternly, stopping him from continuing his assault on the maps with his eyes. Shock flicks across his face at my demand coming out of nowhere. 'You can't plan a battle on no sleep.' It doesn't take much more insisting when he goes to gather his maps.

'No, no maps!' I say, ushering him out of the chamber.

He is a man who will never sleep a wink if it means justice prevails across the entirety of the realm.

Chapter Thirteen

TOM

GREYFALL IS NEVER QUIET, not truly. But this morning, we march, and it feels like the entire realm has stopped breathing. The courtyard below the northern gate swells with motion, but none of it is chaotic. Greyfall's warriors are trained to be a single body; each piece knows its purpose, each motion is carried with precision. They move together, no calls, no hesitation. A gap closes before it can form, a flank turns before it's threatened, no one breaks rank and no one lags behind.

I stand at the edge of it all, one boot braced on the stone ledge that overlooks the final muster. From this height, I can see the sweep of the valley below, white with snow, dark with trees, and far in the distance, the narrow path we will take through the mountains toward Atticus Star.

Lex sits just beneath my skin, still and sharp, ready and excited for what is coming.

Light footsteps sound behind me, deliberate. I know them before I turn. Kira.

I just nod to her, jaw tight, my pulse louder than it has any right to be.

'I'll keep you close,' I say as soon as she is beside me, looking out over the forces as well.

She smirks slightly. 'That's the plan.'

A movement catches my eye beyond the gate. Helios, or well, Lucifer, pacing, his shimmering coat black as night, shifting like shadow with every step. He looks like a storm, an angry, darkened storm, yellow eyes glowing deep and sinister, ready to reduce the enemy to debris.

I look to Kira. 'When the bond calls out there, it won't be about comfort; it's going to be about survival.'

She nods. 'I know.' Her hand reaches out, curling lightly around my wrist.

My blood thumps at her touch; she knows, she can feel the increased excitement in the touch itself.

Not even a moment later, a horn blows. One long, low note carries over the snow-laced grounds. The gates of Greyfall open, and the Lycans begin their march.

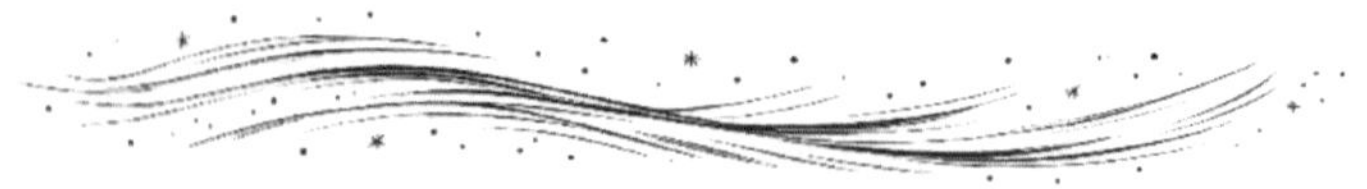

The ridge is quiet, save for the whisper of wind and the low crackling of campfires below. The scent of ash, metal, and anticipation clings to the air. Atticus Star's stronghold lay stretched out beneath us in the basin, its jagged towers and cold spires looming like the bones of something ancient and unforgiving.

Helios stands at the cliff's edge, arms folded tight across his chest, his hair blowing behind him as he looks over the stronghold. His breath fogs in the cold, but his expression doesn't shift. His eyes are fixed below, calculating, but I know him too well to be fooled by his stillness.

I move to stand beside him, my posture loose and alert. Together, we watch the fields and buildings below. On the other side, our Lycans are sharpening weapons, running drills, and reinforcing the perimeter. Every movement is deliberate, disciplined, and heavy with purpose.

'You remember the day you saved me?' Helios asks suddenly.

I arch a brow. 'Which one?'

He gives a huff of something that isn't quite a laugh. 'The first, in Greyfall. As the skinny little orphan rat you were.' He smirks.

I roll my shoulders, watching the clouds gather over the ridgeline. 'Ah, you say that like I've turned into something other than an orphaned rat.'

Helios doesn't look at me. 'You did.'

The silence settled between us again. Below, a scout gives a sharp whistle, signal received, perimeter holding.

'I don't want to lose you here,' Helios says after a while. Quiet and raw. Almost like pulling a tooth and handing it back to the owner.

I don't look at him when I answer, 'You won't.' Then I hesitate for just a breath, 'But if you do… you'd better win this war.'

Helios exhales through his nose, part grim amusement, part grief. 'Oh, believe me, if something happens to you, I'll burn the realm down.'

I believe him; this is a man who has shown me so much dedication and loyalty, considering where I have come from. Only now we are completely connected, deeper than the connections he had with any of the brothers who are no longer walking the realm with us.

As I turn to leave, his voice catches me once again.

'Make sure you tell her what you want after this war. Tell her what you expect for the future.'

I pause, not because I don't know what he means, but because I do.

I can still feel her presence like a heartbeat against mine. Not only because of the bond, though that continues to throb between us, but because she has become a fixed point for me now.

I just nod and walk into the darkness.

The path back to my tent is lined with torches, their flames dancing in the breeze. Warriors pass me without comment; nods are exchanged and shoulders brush in shared understandings. They are ready and focused.

When I reach the edge of camp, Kira is standing outside her tent, arms crossed, face lit by the flicker of the nearby flame. Her hair is braided back and her leathers are tight against her slight frame. She looks up as I approach, and I see the question in her eyes.

'Are we ready?'

I nod, 'As ready as we will ever be.'

'Come in,' she breathes.

The inside of her tent is warm, lit by a small lantern and the heat of her body beside mine. Right now is about being as real as I possibly can. Because tomorrow we march toward uncertainty.

And tonight, we are still whole.

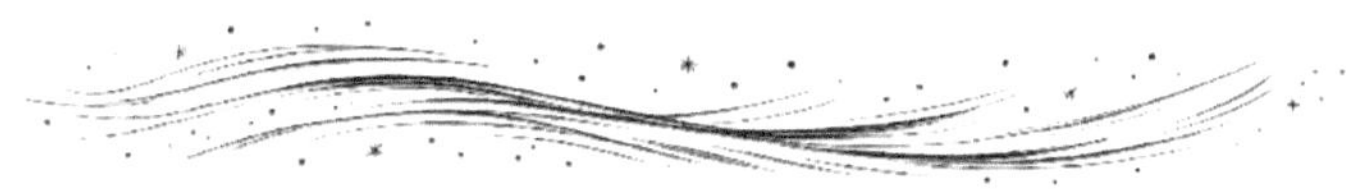

KIRA

The lamp in my tent casts a soft amber glow, flickering the shadows against the canvas walls. It smells of leather and smoke. But Tom's scent quickly fills my senses as he follows me through the flap, coffee and rain. As he comes inside, the tent somehow feels smaller. Quieter.

Our eyes meet across the tent's dim stillness, and in that instant, I feel every moment we have held back crash into the air between us. The war, the fear, the bond, the silence etches into my bones.

Then he moves.

Two strides is all it takes, and his hands are on me, his fingers sliding along my cheeks, holding onto me. His mouth crushing against mine as I rise on my toes to meet him, pulling him closer with desperate fists in the collar of his shirt. The kiss isn't soft or gentle. It is fire, raw, unspoken need and desire.

He lifts me effortlessly, his arms strong around my waist as he backs us toward the furs. Our lips never breaking, his tongue slides against mine, hungry and hot, tasting like sin, and it has never felt so good before.

He lays me down but doesn't hover above me like he might break me. No, he presses into me, his hands mapping my body while his weight on top of me grounds me at the moment. Tom lifts my shirt as I rip his away; we undress each other like starved animals.

There is no patience tonight.

Only need.

Once he has bared my body, his hungry gaze roams all over me. Not for purity, not for beauty, but simple desire. For the scars we both bear and the flesh I have tried to keep to myself for so long.

'Kira,' he breathes, his voice wrecked. 'Tell me you want this.'

I reach for him instantly, my nails scraping lightly down his spine, 'I want you.'

That is all he needs.

He kisses down my throat, across the line of my collarbone, each touch feels like he is lighting a fire beneath my skin. When he finally slides down between my thighs, I am already trembling while the bond hums like a fever between us.

Tom enters me with slow and deliberate force, inch by inch, his eyes locked onto mine the entire time, his hands bracing on either side of me. I gasp, clinging to his shoulders, the stretch of him setting my every nerve on fire.

'Goddess,' I whisper.

Tom groans low in his throat, and he leans down, his head nudging into the marking spot on my neck. 'You feel like home.'

Every thrust is steady, claiming and full of worship from a god in a man's body. The furs tangle beneath my back as my legs wrap around his hips, pulling him into me deeper, harder.

I meet him thrust for thrust, gasps and moans spilling from my lips as pleasure coils tighter and tighter.

'More,' I beg, not ashamed.

He gives me more.

Faster. Rougher. His hand cradles the back of my head while his mouth presses kisses to my temples between his thrusts. I feel him everywhere, and when I cum, it isn't just an orgasm.

The waves roll through my body in a sensation I have never felt before. Ongoing and soul shattering tension fills my body, which trembles uncontrollably. It is the most complete release of every emotion I believe I have ever felt and some which are new to me.

I shatter around him, crying out his name and grabbing onto his hips, not wanting to leave this moment behind. He follows a breath later, spilling into me with a growl of pure, unbroken devotion. His weight drops gently, his arms safely caging me in as his face buries into my neck.

We lay here like this for a long time. Just breathing and connecting with each other.

The weather outside the tent thickens, thunder and cracks of lightning booming through the canvas of the tent. My body, however, hums with warmth, my muscles loose in a way I have never felt before, and my nerves blissfully fried.

Tom shifts, pulling the furs around us, wrapping me up in his arms. I rest my head against his chest, just listening to the slow and steady beat of his heart as it settles

'I want to properly bond with you, Kira,' Tom states bluntly. 'I want you to be mine forever.'

'I want that,' I say honestly. 'More than I ever thought I could.'

Tom kisses me again, this time slow, lingering. The kind of kiss that says he have time. That tomorrow will come and we will survive anything it throws at us.

His lips barely leave mine when he whispers, 'Then stay alive.'

I press my forehead to his, letting the weight of that comment settle between us.

Chapter Fourteen

TOM

THE GATES FALL AT dawn. I feel it before I see it, a tremor through the realm, like the ground itself was holding its breath. Then the war horn cuts through the silence, long, low, and final. A sound meant to summon death. A sound meant to remind every Lycan on the field that we have come not just to fight, but to end the brutality and win.

Lex stirs immediately, already impatient. My body moves before thought can catch up, muscle memory taking over. We've drilled this moment a hundred times, but nothing can prepare you for the sound the timber makes when it shatters under pressure. A groaning, tearing scream that echoes through the air.

The gate of Atticus Star falls into pieces, and the pack that has ruled through fear suddenly has something of their own to fear.

The clashing of claws follows, loud and brutal. Arrows scream overhead, and the first line of Greyfall warriors surges forward like a tide loosed from a dam. I am already halfway down the slope when Lex pushes forward, eager, and I let him come.

The shift hits hard and fast, my bones shattering and knitting back together in an instant, my skin splitting to let Lex out. The world sharpens, the colours brighter, the smells more vivid, like the scent of blood already thick in the air. Lex's paws hit the ground like thunder, and we are in the centre of the chaos.

Complete chaos.

A guard lunges; I meet him mid-air, claws catching his throat, fangs tearing down. His body crumples to the ground. Another to my left, smaller and faster. I twist and pivot on instinct, sinking my teeth into his side and shaking until I hear the unmistakable snap of his ribs.

Blood paints the surrounding snow.

Their alpha is barking orders from the wall, calling for them all to die. But I can smell their hesitation. They aren't ready; they thought their walls would hold; they thought fear would save them. They forgot what true rage looks like when it is fuelled by an actual cause.

I shift back partially, just enough to use my hands, claws still long and my vision still sharp. I rip the sword from a fallen warrior and surge forward, and the first wave breaks through.

We pour through the remains of the gate, Greyfall warriors howling in their victory, their fangs bared, claws gleaming with blood. I am at the front, cutting down anything that stands in our path. My heart thunders in my chest. My breath coming in raggedly. Every movement fuelled by something deeper than the war.

Where is she!?

My gaze keeps moving, face after face, not her.

I turn again. And again, and every face that isn't hers makes my chest tighten, every breath shorter than the last as the tension coils deeper.

Stay close, I told her, these words now echoing back at me. And her reply, *I need to do this,* rings in my ears as I scan the crowd again.

Goddess. Kira. Please.

I slam my shoulder into another warrior, sending him sprawling across the ground. Finishing him, I move on. My claws are slick with blood. My arms are aching, but I don't stop. I can't stop until I find her.

Helios' banner rises above the charge. He is somewhere in the chaos, likely tearing through the command ranks like a god of absolute fury. I can feel his presence the same way I feel the gravity of the mountain we are standing below, unshakable. But even that isn't enough to pull my focus from the single threat running constantly through my mind.

Kira.

I smell her without seeing her.

Peonies. Smoke. And blood.

Not her blood, thank the Goddess.

I turn toward what I think is the east wall, vaulting over a half fallen barricade. And there she is.

She moves like a blade set loose, her smaller form darting between opponents, cutting fast and clean. Her daggers flash, catching the sunlight like fire. She ducks a blow, counters and drives her elbow into a guard's throat, dropping him with terrifying precision.

I watch her kill without hesitation; I watch her move with a kind of fury that comes not from rage, but from purpose.

And I have never loved her more.

A large male, armoured heavily gets behind her, his blade already arcing down at her when I launch myself.

'Kira,' I roar, my voice tearing through the battlefield. She turns, but not fast enough. I catch the bastard mid-swing. We collide in a shower of sparks and blood; I slam him to the ground, my claws raking and teeth snapping. He fights hard. He dies even harder.

When I look up, Kira is standing over me, breathing hard.

Our eyes lock; she doesn't thank me, just nods. We stand back to back after that. And together, we continue tearing Atticus Star down brick by brick.

Chapter Fifteen

TOM

'LEFT FLANK!' HELIOS' VOICE cuts through the clamour, a war cry wrapped in a command. I turn on instinct, in time to see the pack of armoured Atticus Star warriors closing in from the archway. I immediately move to my king.

Helios is already moving, his claws a blur of bloody crimson. He fights like a true monarch, controlled and unyielding. Every motion is efficient and designed to kill. My style is rougher. Lower to the ground. I move like the street wolf I've always been: fast, brutal, and unforgiving.

We fall into a rhythm without thinking; we always do.

Helios sweeps low; I strike high.

He turns; I cover his blind side.

The sickening crunch of bones fills the air. I catch one warrior across the ribs, my claws raking through his side before I throw him to the ground. Another comes from behind; Helios turns, claws arcing through the space where my head had been only moments before.

'Focus,' Helios barks.

'I am,' I snarl back.

He grunts, 'Good, let's finish this.'

We fully shift, Lex and Lucifer surging forward, carving a brutal path through the courtyard. The stone beneath our feet is slick with blood, the snow already trampled to slush beneath the carnage. My heart pounds, not from exhaustion, but from anticipation, from rage.

Every wolf we bring down, I think of the omega boy at the post. Of the council who were so determined not to do anything, to let the injustice continue. Of Kira.

Kira.

A scream rings out, high and sharp, and horrifyingly familiar and I instantly shift back. It cuts through the chaotic scene like an arrow through flesh, and my heart stops.

I turn instantly, scanning the battlefield. For one gut wrenching moment, I can't find her. Just bodies, smoke, and movement.

Another wave of Atticus wolves pours through the gates.

Helios takes one step forward and then pauses. He looks at me, eyes hard, scrutinising.

'Go,' he says, voice like stone. 'Find her.'

I don't say a word, just turn and run.

The smoke is thick and low, choking the stone corridors with ash and fury. It clings to my lungs as my feet slam over the broken ground, cutting through the blood and ruin. I keep running; I can't stop.

Lex howls inside me, a maddening, primal pulse between us. We are both hunting the same thing. The only thing that matters. Kira. He snarls as the bond between us, always a steady drumbeat at the edge of our senses, flickers for the first time since it snapped into place.

The air leaves my lungs.

'No,' I growl, slamming my palm against the stone so hard it split my skin. 'No. Lex. Find her!'

Lex rises, furious and frantic in a half shift, howling into the air around us. He shakes my bones, splits me down the centre; the bond doesn't answer. Or maybe it does, but wrongly. Twisted like someone has snapped it in half.

'She's close,' I pant. 'She has to be.'

But every direction reeks of blood. Of fear. Of wolves, I don't know.

I turn blindly and run. Through side corridors where less fighting hinders my progress, past crumpled bodies and the clang of distance fights. I tear through hallways that stink of pain and rage, my claws scraping the stone, my teeth clenching tightly.

'Kira!'

Silence.

Lex snaps in my head, rabid and wild. He wants out, wants to tear this place apart until it gives her back to us.

I give in to him, teeth and vision sharp.

Fuck.

'Hold on,' I breathe, every step heavy.

She isn't dead; she can't be. I would know, I would have felt it. The bond is faint but not gone.

It feels like the bond is tearing. Not snapping, not breaking cleanly. Tearing. Like claws dragging slowly through my chest,

I skid around the corner and instantly freeze; so much fear flooding my system. The courtyard beyond the archway is wide and circular, torches flaring high against carved stone. And at its centre.

Kira.

She's barely standing, blood running freely from a gash above her brow, streaking down her cheek. But her spine is straight. Her chin lifted. Unbowed.

Alpha Aston stands opposite her, loose and relaxed.

I roar, the sound shaking the walls, causing snow to drop in heavy heaps at the base of the stones.

Helios steps in behind me, a low, dangerous sound building in his chest.

Kira's eyes snap to me. And Goddess—she smiles.

Not soft, not afraid.

Alpha Aston turns slowly, a subtle and calculated shift in his stance, lips curling. 'You came after all.'

Helios moves, and so does Aston, who feints fast, vicious, and underhandedly. His body pivots, claws flashing, not to strike, but to seize.

Helios lunges forward, and I see it too late. Kira.

She moves with no hesitation and no warning, throwing herself between the two of them.

Aston's hand closes, not on Helios… On her.

For half a second, everything stills, even Aston, as though he is shocked at the outcome. Then his lips curl.

'Well,' Alpha Aston drawls, fisting his hand in her hair and yanking her hard against him.

My mind instantly snaps.

An invisible ward slams into place between them and us, violent, absolute. It hits Helios first, hard enough to shake the ground, a snarl ripping from him as his claws rake against nothing.

It slams into me a second later, causing me to fully shift back from Lex, pain exploding up my arms as I try to force through it. But nothing, it doesn't give. We underestimated his warlocks. I strain against the invisible barrier, muscles screaming, vision sharp. 'Let her go.' Alpha Aston laughs.

'She was meant to be my Luna,' he says casually, leaning down and kissing Kira hard, possessively and cruel. She bites him, hard enough to draw blood, but he only chuckles, wiping the blood off his lip with amusement etched on his face.

'Once she learned her place, that is,' he continues, eyes never leaving mine. 'Such a shame. Strong she-wolf. Fiery. I'll miss her warming my bed.'

The world goes silent.

Kira doesn't cry or beg. She just spits blood in his face.

'You'll die screaming,' she says clearly.

Alpha Aston snarls and raises his hand; his claws extend. I slam against the ward as he drives his claws forward, straight through her.

Our bond flares, white-hot, blinding, and then collapses completely.

'No!' The word rips from my throat, primal and broken.

Helios roars and moves from my peripherals, the sound tearing through the courtyard.

Kira gasps, not in fear, but in pain. Her body goes slack, her eyes locking onto mine as the life drains from them. The bond between us screams once and then goes dark.

Something inside me shatters.

The barrier ward between me and Aston explodes inwards, as if it had never existed, and I surge forward.

I hit Alpha Aston with a force that caves in his ribs and pulverises his bones. We slam into the stone dais, the alpha barely having time to snarl before my claws are buried in him.

'There is no place,' I snarl, my voice not entirely my own as Lex rises into me, the two of us synced. 'Where you ever get to even speak her name or think of her again.'

Blood sprays as the alpha screams beneath me, not once but over and over.

Raw animalistic sounds, but I don't kill him yet, not yet. He doesn't deserve the mercy of an easy death.

My claws tear through him again, lower this time, ripping a broken sound from his throat as he thrashes beneath me, hands scrambling, pushing but failing to get me off.

'Please—' It chokes out of him, wet and desperate. Begging from an alpha should amuse me; instead, it just infuriates me.

I lean closer.

'You don't get to beg,' I growl.

He screams again when I drag my claws back through him, slower this time. Deliberately, I want him to feel it. I want him to know I will keep Kira's promise until his last breath; he will die screaming. His voice breaks, splintering into something unrecognisable as he tries to pull away, blood pooling beneath him, soaking into the stone.

'Stop!' he screams, the sound filling my ears, but I don't.

I grip his jaw, forcing his head back, making him look at me. His scream tears through the courtyard as I rip his jaw free from his face.

Even then, when there is nothing left to kill, even as the sound of his scream dies in my ears, I can't stop.

I slam his skull against the stone.

Again. Again. Again.

Until he is unrecognisable and still I claw at him.

Large, rough hands grab me from behind.

'Tom!' Helios roars, bracing his full weight against me. 'Tom, enough!'

I fight. Even against Helios, I fight. Snapping at him.

Helios takes a blow to the shoulder, but without flinching, he wraps his arms around my chest, hauling me back with a grunt of effort.

'He's dead,' Helios says, his voice breaking through the red haze. 'You killed him. It's done.'

I sag into Helios. The rage draining out of me all at once, leaving behind something much, much worse.

Nothing.

I fall to my knees beside Kira's body. Her eyes are still wide open, and with shaky hands, I gently close them.

'I am so sorry,' I whisper, silent tears falling as I press my forehead to hers. 'I should have been faster.'

Helios kneels beside me, one hand heavy on my back. Around us, the courtyard is silent; no one dares to speak.

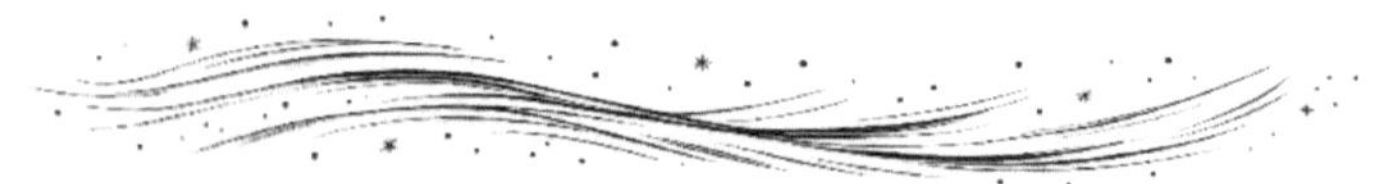

The battlefield is still, too still. Littered with the bodies of the surrounding enemy. The eyes of the warlocks Helios killed to destroy the ward stare into nothing… too late. He wasn't fast enough to save her.

Snow drifts like ash, slow and soft and unsparing, dusting the realm in silence. The bodies have been cleared; the blood has frozen, but the echoes remain.

And now… nothing.

Kira lay in the centre of it all, cloaked in a stillness more profound than death should allow. I stay kneeling beside her, fingers numb, not from the cold, but from what I could no longer feel. The bond.

That invisible tether that had once thrummed like a heartbeat, a lifeline between us, is severed. Quiet now, still, silent and dead.

I reach out slowly and brush my knuckles along her jaw. She is cold beneath my touch. Not icy, just absent. The heat that had once radiated from her like a wildfire is gone out. The fire she's always carried, even in her fear, even in defiance, gone.

'I don't know how to do this,' I murmur. The words drift into the wind, and no answer comes back.

I exhale shakily and look at her again, really looking. Not as the warrior she has been, not as the mate I loved. But as the girl I first saw in the clearing. Bloodied, furious and unbroken.

I remember every scar she has shown me and every smile she never meant to give. Every night she was strong enough to choose to stay, even when I know she wanted to run. And the very last time she freely kissed me, really, truly kissed me.

The other Lycans stay back. No one interrupts. I lean forward and press my forehead against Kira's once again, my lips barely brushing her skin. But I don't say goodbye. I can't say goodbye.

Above, the stars blaze cold and beautiful.

I imagine her among them, wild and free, untouched by the chains of any man, any pack, and the past.

'Rest, Kira,' I whisper.

Chapter Sixteen

TOM

I SIT BESIDE HER all night. I don't move. I don't speak.

The others come and go, soft-footed and quiet, but I barely notice any of them. I only see her. Laid out on the cold stone bench like a fallen warrior, her hands folded gently over her chest, the tips of her fingers brushing a silver wolf charm someone else has placed there. A token of protection, maybe. Someone's farewell, I don't know who left it, but I am grateful. It feels right for her to have.

The fires went out hours ago. The last candle sputters in the far corner, its light flickering over the dark strands of her hair. It dances in the curls at her temple; the lashes resting against her cheeks. Goddess, she looks peaceful.

I've fought in many battles, lost brothers and strangers. I've held bleeding men in my arms and felt the last breath leave their lungs. But this, the silence, the emptiness in the space where she should be breathing right beside me, it's hollowed something out of me.

I changed as soon as we returned to Greyfall. Black now being a more suitable choice than ever. My hands, however, are still stained red with blood. Not hers. But I haven't washed them. I couldn't. It feels like a betrayal to wipe away the night when Kira will never see another morning with me.

The others prepared her body with care. None of them have known her long, but they knew exactly what she meant. What she changed, and even the king himself stood over her, head bowed, saying nothing.

She was the beginning of something massive, of full-blown liberation. She showed us the truth in the north, and now she is also the end of something massive.

I sit here with my elbows on my knees, fingers loosely knotted together, staring at the scar on her bottom lip. I can't help my eyes consistently running over all the features of her face, memorising them, committing them to memory for the rest of my life.

Hundreds of omegas are free now because of her. The packs are shifting; the outcome grew Greyfall's position to the north, and all the laws and councils are changing. They need to; they cannot survive Helios if they don't. He is making sure Kira's sacrifice is not for nothing. He is making sure it is, instead, her legacy.

My hand drifts towards hers, hovering just above it. I don't touch her; I just can't seem to bring myself to feel the stillness. Like touching her now will shatter the emotional barrier I have crafted so thoroughly.

But Goddess, I want to feel her skin one last time. I want to memorise the shape of her fingers, the curve of her palm, and the way her hand would hold mine without hesitation. I can't help but think of the way she looked at me that last night in the tent. Like I was someone she had finally chosen, not because of our fate, not because she was desperately seeking protection, but simply because I was the one she wanted. I was the one she chose to trust.

Kira kissed me like it meant something, like it would last. And I… I let myself believe it would, that I had finally found the happily ever after all the other Lycans find.

Now, silence is all I have.

I lean back slowly, resting against the back of the stone bench. My eyes burn, but I don't blink. Don't cry, the tears feel stuck somewhere behind my ribs, locked in the cage within my chest. If I cry, It's real. If I cry, everything I ever wanted is over.

Instead, I breathe. In and out. Slow and measured, as though if I just keep breathing, I can anchor her here to me, in spirit. If I hold this vigil long enough, she will wake and tell me how overdramatic I am being. How I need to stop moping around.

The candle dies with a final hiss. And the darkness swallows us both.

Chapter Seventeen

TOM

WE BURY HER BENEATH the starlight tree at the northern edge of the homestead's grounds.

It has always been sacred ground, even before I knew what sacred really meant. It was not a place for us pups to play, and whenever we attempted to approach; we were immediately turned away at every angle, not just the direct route. It's the kind of place you don't speak, not necessarily because of any rules, but because the entire space around the tree demands silence and respect. The wind even moves quieter now; the soil feels softer, deeper, and older. Like it remembers everything and everyone who touches it.

The tree itself is ancient, older than any wolf alive today. Its bark is dark and rough, cracked with silver veins that shimmer in the moonlight. They say the Moon Goddess wept here, long ago, when her mate was ripped from her. That her tears watered the roots and made them sacred, and that when a soul worthy of absolute remembrance returns to the earth beneath the tree, it will fill with white blooms.

It hasn't bloomed in my lifetime; not many are committed to the earth up here anymore.

But I carry her there. My arms don't shake; my legs don't falter. Not because I am strong, but because I can't let them, not for this, not for Kira.

She is wrapped in a pale grey cloth, her body weighing nothing and everything all at once, like I am carrying the very last of the world's warmth in my arms. The walk from the chamber to the tree takes a lifetime, almost like the tree is not getting closer no matter how many steps I take. Or maybe it was that time moves differently when I have her in my arms. Every step I am taking is a memory with her, every breath that catches in my throat is turning into screams I can't let out. Lycans and wolves line the path from all walks of life: warriors, healers, elders, and omegas. Some I have fought beside, others I have never met, but all of them bow their heads as I pass. But no one speaks.

Not even Helios. He walks behind me silently. Even the priests, old and cloaked in the moon's thread, say nothing, no rites or blessings as befitting the sacred tree.

The ground is already broken when we arrive, softened by magic and shovels. The grave isn't deep, but it is enough. Enough to hold her body. It will never be enough, however, to hold everything that she was. I step down into the hollow myself; my knees sinking into the damp earth; my hands shake only once when I lay her down.

I don't rush as I smooth the cloth wrapping her. This has to be perfect.

I climb out of the grave only when I can't bear the sight of her stillness any longer.

Helios takes the first shovel of earth. He doesn't look at me, just tosses it into the grave with the weight of a king burying one of his own.

I take the second. Each scoop of soil sounds wrong; final and heavy. It hits her body like soft drumbeats, one after another, until she disappears beneath it.

The snow has stopped now, but the cold is pressing closer. When the last layer of soil is smoothed and shaped with careful hands, I step forward again, falling to one knee.

I sit in silence as the crowd thins. I watch as wolves and Lycans bow once more, then turn and walk away, leaving only footprints and the flickering lanterns behind. Even Helios leaves eventually, though his hand rested on my shoulder before he did, brief and strong.

I stay.

Until it is just me, the tree, and her grave. The wind whispers through the branches, stirring the silver-threaded bark. I can still smell her if I think hard enough. Beneath the scent of snow, pine and earth, there is still the faint hint of peony. All that remains of the bond we had barely begun to understand.

As I watch the base of the tree, where her head now lies, something small unfurls.

A bloom. White and soft, a single flower, its petals curling inward. The first bloom the tree has offered in decades. I stare at it, breath caught somewhere between awe and anguish. Reaching out, my fingertips brush along the edge of it. It doesn't wither or shrink from my touch. It simply sways. And finally, it all bubbles up. I let myself feel the impact, my vision blurring as tears stream down my face, warm and unstoppable. No sounds, no dramatic heaving sobs, just warm, endless tears that fall down my face into the collar of my shirt as I kneel in the snow. My hand presses into the soil, fingers curling like I can still reach her, the only part of me I wanted to keep whole.

I stay until the moon crests the treetops and the lanterns have burned low. Until the bloom at the base of the tree is joined by a second. And a third.

Then I stand.

Not because I want to leave, but because I know she would hate the idea of me wasting away beside her. She didn't fight her way to freedom just to tie me to ruin. I press my palm to the bark and hold it there until my fingers stop shaking. Until it anchors me.

Then I turn toward the path and walk back into a world without her.

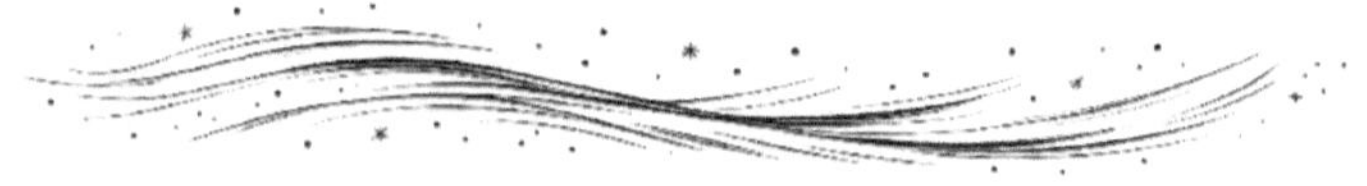

I survive the night.

It takes me two days to go back to her room. I stop outside the door longer than I mean to, but then it opens too easily when I turn the handle. The room still smells of her. Not blood or battlefield, just her. Peonies, moonlight, and warmth.

When the door first opens, the air hits me like a physical blow to the chest. No one has touched anything; Helios had made sure of that. The truth is, I miss her. For a second, I expect to hear her laugh.

The silence that follows is worse.

The blanket it still tossed over the chair like she'd dropped it mid-thought. Her clothes are folded with the same sharp efficiency that only she had, and there is a cup on the desk with a faint pink mark on the rim—her lips.

My hand lingers on the back of her chair, fingers tightening against the wood, hand trembling. I move through the room slowly, touching things as I pass: her desk, the edge of the bed, unsure of what I am searching for. Maybe something to anchor me here, maybe a sign or a piece of her I can keep with me.

Restlessness is a savage trait for an orphan, but also a very standard one. But today, I want nothing but rest. I sink into the bed and curl into her furs, pulling them tight around me; her scent is still here. I breathe it in, again and again, until my chest stops feeling like it might split open.

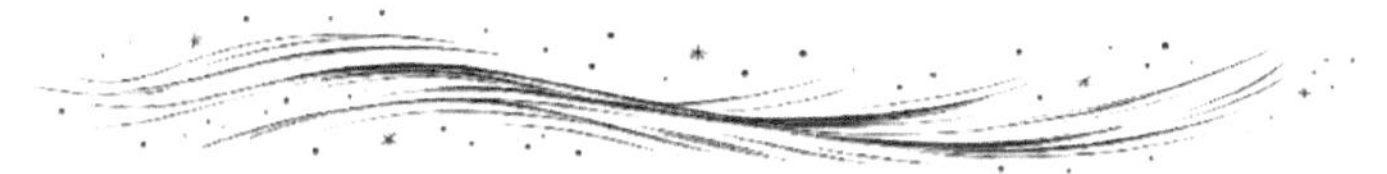

The dream comes like snowfall, slow, silent, and pure.

I don't feel it immediately, not the cold, not the shift, just the quiet that is abundantly clear around me now. Then the silence deepens, expands almost. It isn't empty; it's full of starlight, with a breath and a heartbeat belonging to something older and wiser than myself.

I stand beneath the burial tree. Its trunk shimmering silver, veins of light twisting through the bark like moonlight poured into the wood. The branches stretch toward the stars above me, stars that are pulsing too brightly. The entire field glows with an impossible stillness.

I am barefoot; the wind kisses my skin, soft and cool, and when I look up, the moon hangs low in the sky, massive, luminous, and ever watching.

Then I hear her.

'Tom.' Her voice doesn't echo; it vibrates in my chest, in my very soul.

I turn instantly, and there she is.

Kira.

Not broken, not ghostlike. Just unmistakably… her.

Standing there in a soft grey dress that shimmers like the starlight surrounding us, her hair loose and wild around her shoulders. No bruises or scars, her skin glowing, kissed by moonlight, and her eyes, Goddess, her eyes look like they did the first day she dared to meet mine. Unafraid. Alive!

I can't breathe. This is a nasty trick.

I move, half in disbelief, half in desperation, but she is already taking steps forward. We meet in the middle of the dream field, and our foreheads touch like it is the only thing in the world that still makes sense.

Warm. Real. Steady.

Her hands slide up my chest. Mine find her waist. We don't speak for a long moment.

Then she whispers, 'I don't have long.'

My throat tightens. 'Is this real?'

Kira pulls back just enough to meet my eyes. Her smile is soft.

'Real enough.'

I can't stop the grief from rising, suffocating and sharp, like it is hitting me fresh all over again.

'I should've saved you,' I say. My voice sounds raw.

Her fingers brush my cheek. 'You gave me everything. You helped me see that I deserved a future, and most of all that I deserved justice.'

'It wasn't enough.' I say, tears pricking the edges of my eyes.

'It was more than I ever dreamed I could have.' She says it like a blessing, almost like forgiveness. But it cracks me open all the same.

I step back slightly, needing so badly to see her fully—as if memorising her all over again here, like this, will let me hold on to her longer.

'I don't belong to the world anymore,' she says. Her voice has become softer. 'But you do.'

I shake my head, jaw clenching. 'I don't know how to lead without you. How to breathe without you.' Her smile breaks my heart.

'You do,' she whispers. 'You just don't want to.' She is right.

The silence stretches between us again; not awkward, just there. Filled with meaning we haven't found the words for. The wind moves through the field, a low, rhythmic pulse of the universe breathing in and out.

Then the moon brightens, like a veil lifting.

And her voice shifts again. Like it isn't hers anymore.

'The Moon does not punish with loss.'

I freeze. The words curl around my ribs like vines, gentle but unyielding.

'She balances. Where one flame dies, another will kindle.' The ethereal voice continues. The field is feeling slightly warmer as it does. Brighter possibly.

'Your grief is not the end, Tom.' Kira steps forward, her face fierce, full of something holy. 'It is your beginning.'

Her words wash through me, almost opening up my chest, allowing me to breathe properly again, allowing something through—light and air and strength I haven't let myself feel since I watched her drop before me.

Kira reaches up and presses her lips to my forehead. The bond doesn't flare like I stupidly hoped that it would, and when she pulls back; the field is already fading. The stars are blurring and the wind is now non-existent. Kira's outline turns to light, but her eyes remain steady as ever. 'Another will come, Tom, not in the way you seek, but you will find meaning with him and her both. You will find happiness again.'

And then she is gone. I stand alone beneath the tree again, but not empty.

I wake with a start and tears on my face, her name lightly on my lips.

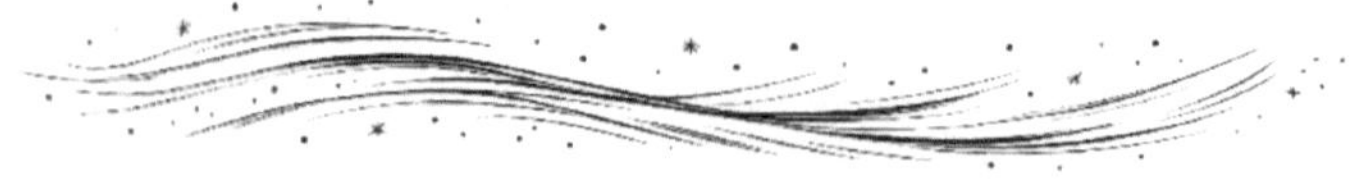

Dawn is breaking over Greyfall. The horizon is burning slowly, deep rose bleeding into amber, and gold spilling like fire across the blanket of snow. Each breath feels cleaner and sharper. Every exhale rises like smoke in the morning light, and for the first time in what feels like forever, I feel something I can't name.

By the time I reach the central homestead from visiting the burial tree, which is now laden with white blooms, Helios is already standing outside the main gates, arms crossed, hair wind swept in the early light.

He says nothing, just looks at me, and I see it in his eyes.

'She came to me,' I say, my voice quiet.

His expression doesn't change; he just nods.

I draw a breath of the cold morning air.

And this time, it doesn't hurt.

The Light Realm
Frost Fang Pack
Iron Blow Pack
Atticus Star Pack
Greyfall
Ravenhill Pack
Dreamshire Pack
Crystal Lake Pack
Sixth Body Pack
Whispering Night Pack

About The Author:
Em J Bakker

Em J Bakker is a passionate romance writer currently based in Victoria, Australia, where she draws inspiration from the natural beauty of the countryside. With a deep love for romantic narratives, both in her own life with her doting partner and within the pages she reads and writes.

Embracing an eclectic writing style, Em J Bakker's projects span from light-hearted comedic romances to gripping dark tales of underworlds. Her writing reflects a blend of creativity nurtured by the serene landscapes and outdoor adventures she enjoys, including days on the lake, exploration of snowfields, and off-road journeys through picturesque terrain alongside her family.

In addition to writing, Em is an avid reader, painter, & pretty rock collector. She finds solace in the pages of a good book and joy in creating artwork using a various of mediums with her young children.

Consistently looking to improve herself, Em engages in various study pursuits, always eager to learn and grow both personally and professionally. Her commitment to self improvement and her diverse hobbies enrich her writing, making her stories vibrant and full of life.

Other Titles By Em J Bakker

The Queen Series:

Book One: Blindsided

Book Two: Fight For Me

Book Three: Rise As One

Novella: The Beta's Price

Novella (in progress): The Broken Moon's Void